Catherine was _____ _____ ...dnight. But when the clock chimed one, she let out a huff and threw the covers off of her so she could cross the room and go to the door connecting their bedchambers. He better not be out with someone else tonight. It was bad enough she had to marry him, but to be deserted on her wedding night in favor of another bed partner made her blood boil with rage. Of all nights, this was the one reserved for her. Her resolve strengthened, she flung the door open and entered his room.

To her surprise, he'd been asleep. He bolted up in his bed, his hair ruffled and his eyes wide. "I don't want to fence!" He blinked in the moonlight and rubbed his eyes. "Where am I?"

Seeing that as her cue, she rushed forward and stood by his bed. "Not with me, which is where you're supposed to be. Do I have to tell you what you're supposed to do on your wedding night?"

"I...uh..." He blinked several more times and stared at her. "I didn't think you'd want me to be with you tonight."

What did her wants have to do with anything? Her duty was to give him an heir. Exasperated, she sighed. "When were you planning on coming to my bed?"

He shrugged. "I don't know."

"You don't know!"

Could he really be so daft that he had no plan? She placed her hands on her hips and glared at him, but the effect was probably lost on him since it was dark and he couldn't see much of her. Inspired, she went to his table and lit a candle. There. Now that he could properly see her disgust, she hurried back over to him and glared at him once more.

He rolled his eyes. "I was doing it for you. I thought you wouldn't want me in your bed, given how much you loathe me."

"This has nothing to do with how I feel about you."

"It doesn't?"

"No, it doesn't. We have a duty to the crown."

He groaned and placed his head in his hands. "You sound just like my mother."

Too annoyed to be nervous, she grunted and pulled her shift off. "I don't care if I sound like her or not. We're going to get this over with." She picked up his covers and nudged him in the side. "Move over so I can get in. I'll go back to my bed once you're done."

***

A Most Unsuitable Earl

A Most Unsuitable Earl

Ruth Ann Nordin

Dedication: To Carol Oberwager-Spencer, your words of encouragement still mean a lot to me. Thanks!

List of Books by Ruth Ann Nordin

Regency Collection
The Earl's Inconvenient Wife
Her Counterfeit Husband
A Most Unsuitable Earl

Nebraska Historical Romance Collection
Her Heart's Desire
A Bride for Tom
A Husband for Margaret
Eye of the Beholder
The Wrong Husband
Shotgun Groom
To Have and To Hold
His Redeeming Bride
Isaac's Decision

South Dakota Historical Romances
Loving Eliza
Bid for a Bride
Bride of Second Chances

Native American Romance Series (historical)
Restoring Hope
Brave Beginnings
Bound by Honor, Bound by Love
A Chance In Time (novella) – main characters show up in Restoring Hope and Bound by Honor, Bound by Love)

Virginia Brides Series (historical)
An Unlikely Place for Love
The Cold Wife
An Inconvenient Marriage
Romancing Adrienne

Other Historical Western Romances
Falling In Love With Her Husband
Meant To Be

Contemporary Romances
With This Ring, I Thee Dread
What Nathan Wants

Across the Stars Trilogy (contemporary)
Suddenly a Bride
Runaway Bride (coming soon)
His Abducted Bride (coming soon)

Chapter One

April 1815

"When are you going to find a respectable young lady to marry?"

Ethan Silverton, the Lord of Edon, looked up from his book in time to see his very unhappy mother enter his library. He slammed the book shut and slid it under his chair before she realized he'd been reading Shakespeare.

She glanced at where he put the book and made the sign of the cross. "You'll be the death of me yet. I don't even want to know what you're reading. If only you'd read one of the books your father invested money in." She gave a mournful sigh and scanned the many books lining the shelves.

"Mother, please. You know I find history and the like boring." He grimaced. Truly, he did. History, biography, politics… They only served one purpose: to put a gentleman to sleep.

She set her plump frame in the chair across from him and wrung her hands. "You were mentioned in the *Tittletattle* again."

His ears perked up at the mention of the scandalsheets. "I was?"

"Don't act so pleased."

He stopped smiling and gave her a solemn nod. "You're

right. I have behaved abhorrently." After a pause, he added, "What did I get caught doing?"

She let out a cry and pressed her hand to her forehead.

"Oh come now, Mother. It couldn't have been that bad."

"It's got to be one of the worst things you've done yet. Prostitutes and your own mistresses are one thing, but you were caught with Lord Hedwrett's mistress…and in broad daylight where everyone could see you!"

"It wasn't like that."

"No?"

"No. It was twilight."

She let out another cry. "Why can't you settle down with a good, respectable lady? Why must you insist on dallying with such…such…women?"

His brown eyes grew wide. "I've never heard you talk this way."

"I'm sorry, Ethan, but you bring out the worst in me. When your father died, I promised him that I would make sure you got an heir. Only, there is no good lady and no son." She gave him a hesitant look. "At least no legitimate son. Are there illegitimate sons?"

"No. I don't think so. At least no one's mentioned it."

"Please, please marry a good lady this Season."

He ruffled his blond hair and groaned. "I've been trying."

"Not hard enough."

"I've been going to each Season for five years."

"And with each passing year, it's getting harder and harder to convince a proper lady that you're worth marrying. As much as ladies desire a titled gentleman, they still have their limits."

Crossing his legs, he leaned back in the chair and watched her as she agonized over his future. He knew she meant well, but the responsibility of the title never appealed to him. How he wished he could hand it over to his cousin who could then take over the estate so he could live a quiet life—out of the limelight—

in his cottage. What more did a gentleman really need than the solitude of good books and the peacefulness of nature? No, instead, he was expected to run from one social event to another and frequent White's. At least in the winter, he could return to Kestrel. But no. It was time to be in London and do the whole running to and fro thing all over again.

Inspired, he straightened. "I have a wonderful idea!"

Though she seemed hesitant, she asked, "You do?"

"Let's give my title to Clarence. You know he'll do well with it!"

"Not this again."

"But why not?"

"It's not as easy as you think it is to hand over your title to him, and if it were, I would forbid it. It's an honor to have one. You shouldn't make light of it."

He sunk back into the chair. He knew she was going to say that. She always said that. No matter what vile thing he pulled, she clung to her obsession that he'd pass on the title to a future heir.

"There's a ball tomorrow night," she began, and he groaned. "Now don't act that way, Ethan. I want you to put on your best clothes and be charming to the ladies." She paused for a moment. "Not too charming, mind you. I don't want you to lure an innocent out to the gardens. Granted, a scandal would secure a marriage, but you've lived so recklessly, my heart can't take that kind of betrothal. What we need is an honorable engagement to an honorable lady."

This wasn't the first time she'd made such a declaration, and he was sure it wouldn't be the last. But either way, it wouldn't matter. He was very careful to avoid anything that might mean he had to marry a lady. No one insisted on marriage if the lady in question was a mistress or a lady of ill repute. They were, by far, the safer bet if he felt inclined to talk to a member of the fairer sex.

"I'll attend the ball," he said because he knew it would make her happy. Never mind the fact that she'd be disappointed tomorrow evening when there was no lady who would be a possible daughter-in-law. Just the hope alone would have to suffice.

Relaxing, she smiled. "Thank you. Maybe this Season will be the one!"

Maybe it would be the Season where she would give up her nonsense of him finding a wife.

Standing up, she motioned to the book under his chair. "I'll let you return to," she sighed, "your reading."

His eyebrows arched as he watched her leave. Once she shut the door, he picked up the book and resumed reading. He could only imagine the talk of the Ton if anyone found out he was reading something so noble as Shakespeare. Such a thing wouldn't be good at all to his stellar reputation as a rake.

***

"I'm doomed to be a spinster," Lady Catherine Morgan lamented as she examined her reflection in the mirror. "Nothing you can do will work."

She turned from her vanity, unable to look at herself anymore. What was the use? She already knew why none of the gentlemen had taken an interest in her. Her curly reddish blonde hair was pleasant enough, but it was the only thing on her that made her stand out. She wasn't ugly, but she wasn't pretty either. She was somewhere in the middle. The same was true for her figure. The corset helped to bring out her curves, but her breasts still appeared smaller and her hips a little wider than desired. Nothing, however, could compensate for her most undesirable trait of all: her lack of personality.

Opal, her lady's maid, put the last pin in her hair. "You mustn't give up. Sometimes it takes a while to find a husband."

"Yes, but in my case, 'a while' is an eternity. My only consolation is that I'm my father's daughter instead of his son. I'd hate to think the fate of the title rested on my shoulders."

"You're much too nervous when it comes to social events. Go there to have a good time."

Opal didn't understand. But how could she? She was a lady's maid, not the daughter of a duke. "Sometimes I envy you. You don't have to go to balls and hope that this will be the night you can finally meet the gentleman who'll marry you so your father will feel better about your future."

"His Grace is a good gentleman. He wants to see you happy."

"Yes, I know." And she couldn't fault him for that. "Please don't try to console me anymore, Opal. I know you mean well, but my course has been set. There is no good in denying it."

With a sigh, Opal put the pins away. "I understand your plight, my lady, but I assure you that these things happen when you least expect it."

"You're very kind to say that." Opal had said the same thing last year, and though at the time Catherine thought she might be right, this time she held a much more pessimistic point of view.

"Come, my lady, the guests will be here soon."

Reluctant, Catherine rose to her feet. Her satiny-silver dress swirled around her feet. A panel of ruffles enhanced the skirt and her inserted waist made of black fabric accented the gown. The dress had a low neckline, and she wore a bronze necklace and earrings to match.

Had this been her first Season, she would have felt like a princess. But as she studied her reflection one last time, she felt more like a lady on the brink of spinsterhood. All the dress did was wave a banner begging for someone to marry her. It glittered and shone, but it did nothing else.

Sighing, she left her bedchamber and headed down the

stairs where her father was talking to the butler. She put on a smile because she didn't want her father to know how much she dreaded another Season. He'd been so kind to her.

He turned his gaze to her and his lips curled up. "Catherine, you look lovely tonight. I knew that dress would be perfect for you." He gave her arm a friendly pat and added, "You look just like your mother."

"I wish I remembered her."

"She'd be proud of you and the fine young lady you've become."

She'd like to think so. From time to time, she'd go to her father's library and study her mother's portrait. He had it done shortly after their marriage, so she was still in full health. A year after she was born, her mother grew ill, and within two months, she passed away. There were times when she yearned for her, and right now, she thought her mother might be the only one who'd understand her situation.

"Catherine," her father began, interrupting her thoughts, "let's go to the ballroom and wait for the guests. I need to make sure the orchestra is ready."

Nodding, she followed him and examined the ballroom. Her dear father had spared no expense for the evening. Every candle in the chandeliers was lit. The orchestra waited in the balcony above the room to play. An elaborate assortment of foods and drinks rested on the tables. The entire place was decorated with all the pageantry that would make even Lady Cadwalader green with envy.

She couldn't help but feel sorry for her father. He was doing everything he could to attract a respectable nobleman for her, and she feared it was all for nothing. No. Tonight was going to end as all the other nights had. There would be no suitor. Her father would be disappointed. She'd end up telling herself that being without a husband wasn't the worst thing that could happen to her. In fact, given enough time, she might even be content.

But deep down, she didn't believe she'd ever be content unless she had a husband and children. And that made her think of herself as the most pitiful lady of all.

***

Ethan took care to pull the cloak further over his head so no one would see him as he made his way down the street. He didn't have much time. In half an hour, his mother would expect him to be at the ball the Duke of Rumsey was hosting. It was ridiculous that he was a grown gentleman who still had to obey the demands of his mother. But his mother was a good lady. He couldn't fault her for trying to get him married. She was doing what any concerned mother would do.

Lowering his head so Lord and Lady Roderick wouldn't notice him as their carriage passed by, he hurried his pace and turned the corner of the next street. He made sure no one was in sight then ran up the steps to the townhouse. He knocked on the door, using his usual three taps and waited a second before adding two more so the owner would know it was him.

He waited for a few seconds before Agatha Lyons, the Lady of Richfield, opened the door. She gasped and pulled him inside. Before he had a chance to greet her, she shoved him into the drawing room and motioned for him to hide behind the door. He obliged and waited as the footman walked down the hallway.

"My lady, why did you answer the door?" the footman asked in a baffled tone.

Agatha cleared her throat and laughed. "I wasn't answering the door. I thought I saw a rat and ran to go outside. I opened the door and it scurried right on out of here. I got so scared that I tripped and fell against the door. That's why you thought you heard someone knocking."

"A rat was in this townhouse?"

"Yes. A big, hairy one. It was disgusting. I still get

shivers when I think about it."

"Hmm. Perhaps I ought to do a search to make sure there's not another one."

"Yes," she replied. "That would be best."

Ethan had to bite down on his tongue so he wouldn't burst out laughing. Leave it to Agatha to come up with such a silly story.

Her footsteps approached the drawing room, and the footman called out, "Shall I check that room before you go in there?"

"Oh," she began, "there's no need. That room is fine."

"How can you be sure?"

"Because it came out of there. Everyone knows that only one rat will be in one place at a time. If there are any more rats, then they'll be in other rooms."

"I haven't heard that rats go alone in rooms. I'm sure they can travel in groups," the footman argued.

"No. The latest research proves otherwise."

"The latest research?"

"This was a 'loner rat'. It's a different type of rat. You can tell them by the white streak on their backs."

"A white streak on their backs?"

Ethan pressed his hand over his mouth, hoping his laughter wouldn't expose her lie. Not only was she lying, but she was horrible at it. A 'loner rat' indeed! Thankfully, she was better at writing for the *Tittletattle* than she was lying about rats.

"Yes," Agatha insisted. "I demand you go look for the other rats in the other rooms."

"Yes, my lady."

Once the footman headed down the hallway, Agatha hurried into the drawing room, startling Ethan who nearly tripped as she shut the door. "Why are you here?" she whispered. "Aren't you supposed to be at the Duke of Rumsey's ball?"

"I'm on my way there," he whispered.

"You couldn't talk your mother out of it?"

He caught the sympathy in her voice and groaned. "She's determined that I marry someone."

"I don't know what else I can do for you. I thought for sure that bit about you and Lord Hedwrett's mistress would've given your poor mother a heart attack."

"She didn't like it," he admitted, "but it hasn't dissuaded her from the lofty dream of seeing me married off and having an heir."

"I still don't understand why you protest the idea so much."

"It's complicated."

She rolled her eyes. "I'm sure."

"Well, I don't see you rushing off to get married since your husband died three years ago."

She shrugged and crossed her arms. "A widow is offered more freedom than a married lady, and I happen to like it."

"Then it seems we are in agreement that freedom is important to both of us."

"I hate it when you make sense. All right. What else do you want me to do?"

He thought over her question carefully. "I'm not sure."

She grumbled.

"What would be something about a gentleman that would convince you he's not worth marrying?"

With a sigh, she paced the floor, her hands behind her back and her head bowed. "Well, you have a title, and as much as you try to lose your wealth, you can't."

"No, I can't." And he tried—oh how he tried!—when he gambled with the other gentlemen. "I don't know how I get so unfortunate."

"Unfortunate?" She shook her head. "You, my lord, are not unfortunate, and that's part of your problem."

"What if you put in the *Tittletattle* that I really don't have any money?"

"Lack of money won't dissuade some ladies from pursuing you."

"Even if I have to forage for food from nearby farms? Write in the *Tittletattle* that I eat pigs' slop."

She giggled but clasped her hands over her mouth so she wouldn't arouse the servants' suspicions. When her laughter died down, she swatted his arm. "I can't do that, and you know it."

"Of course you can. The more absurd something is, the more it'll scare ladies everywhere."

"Some ladies wouldn't mind eating pigs' slop if it meant they could be a countess."

"Surely, you jest!" What lady in her right mind would agree to live like a filthy animal? He shuddered. If he was a lady, he'd go off running in the other direction from such a gentleman. "It'll work. Mention that I borrow my clothes from a family member who pities me. I have to beat the clothes on rocks because I can't afford enough soap. You can even mention that my hair is fake."

"No one will believe any of those things. You're one of the finest dressed gentlemen around."

"Which you can say is my cousin's doing since he buys clothes for me. He's a gentleman of great taste and quite generous."

"And you, my lord, are a gentleman who's utterly charming. Despite yourself, you're an ideal husband."

He grimaced. "I am relieved you have no desire to marry again or I'd be in trouble."

After tapping her foot for a few seconds, she let out a long sigh. "All right. I'll put something into the *Tittletattle* about your lack of funds, but I won't add in the pig slop or the part about your clothes being washed with rocks."

"Thank you. You are the most wonderful lady a gentleman can have the fortune of knowing."

"You remember that when I need you to submit my next

book to the publisher."

"I will. I promise." He pulled the hood of his cloak over his head. "Let me know when it's safe for me to leave." He hid behind the door.

"Ethan, in the future, please use the servants' stairs. I might not always make it to the front door before the footman."

"I will do as you request." He bowed and motioned toward the door. "Is it safe for me to leave?"

She opened the door and peered into the hallway. Glancing back at him, she waved him forward. Taking his cue, he hurried past her and slipped out of the house as quietly as one of the rats she claimed to have seen. He breathed a sigh of relief as he made his way down the street. With any luck, this would be the last ball he'd ever have to attend.

Chapter Two

Catherine twirled around then faced her dance partner. She had no idea what to say to him. He talked extensively about Hyde Park, and she did her duty as a lady, nodding and smiling at the appropriate times. But it wasn't good enough. She could see the disinterest in his eyes and knew he was rambling just to have something to say so there wouldn't be the awful lingering silence between them. All he could do was wait for the music to end so he could find another lady to dance with.

She glanced at her father who stood to the side of the room, mingling with available gentlemen and trying to select a good one for her. She didn't know whether to scream or sigh in frustration. No matter how many gentlemen he tried to match her up with, it wouldn't do any good.

The dance, mercifully, came to an end. She curtsied to her partner and took a reprieve at one of the chairs. She opened her fan, more eager to have something to do with her hands instead of cooling herself off. She really hated balls. Everyone else was having a wonderful time. Why couldn't she? If only she could figure out what to say, she might be able to join in the fun.

Laughter from a group of gentlemen caught her attention, so she glanced over at Lord Edon and those who surrounded him. She couldn't hear what he was saying, but his audience burst into another round of laughter. When he bowed and left the group, she noticed that the gentlemen were disappointed he hadn't stayed longer. As much as she loathed to admit it, she couldn't help but envy him. He fit in so well in a social gathering. How did he do it?

She'd danced with him on several occasions. He was in no way a potential husband. Her father would never approve, and she had no interest in him. She'd much rather live the rest of her life as a spinster than be with someone like him. But he certainly had a gift for attracting people. Not wishing to dwell on how much she envied him such a gift, she turned her attention away from him.

"Lady Catherine, why are you sitting over here where no one can see you?"

Catherine looked up at Lady Roderick who was smiling at her. Blushing, Catherine waved her fan. "I became unbearably warm."

Lady Roderick sat in the chair beside her. "I dread large gatherings."

Surprised, she turned toward her. Lady Roderick was beautiful with her dark hair and olive complexion, and from the few times Catherine had spoken to her, she struck her as a nice lady. So why would she dread the balls? "May I ask why?"

Lady Roderick opened her fan and waved it. "For one, dancing makes me hot, too."

"I think it's because of all the people in the room."

"Probably. But at times, it's overwhelming. Sometimes I feel as if the walls are closing in around me, and when I do, I need to find a quiet place to rest."

"Like now?"

Lady Roderick nodded.

"Then why do you come to balls?" She waved her fan again. "You're already married."

With a chuckle, she replied, "It's because I'm married that I go to them. My husband enjoys political talk, and when we're in

London, balls are one of the places he can talk to other gentlemen who share his interest. I don't mind it, really. My sister and her husband love balls, so it's also a good way to see her. However," leaning forward and lowering her voice, she added, "my husband is helping his friend find a wife, but don't tell anyone I told you that."

"Really? Gentlemen have trouble finding someone to marry?"

"Some do. Are you acquainted with Lord Clement?"

Catherine thought of all the gentlemen she'd met that evening, and most were familiar to her but not that one. "I've heard the name, but I wouldn't know him if I saw him."

"He has a cane."

"Oh him! Yes, I remember him, but I haven't made his acquaintance."

"He prefers not to dance because of his limp."

"One can hardly blame him."

"If you'd like, I could arrange it so that he comes over," Lady Roderick suggested. "He's terribly nice but easily overlooked."

Her face warmed. "I don't know…"

"Do you wish to get married?"

Catherine took a deep breath and licked her lips. "Yes."

"Well, Lord Clement is one of the finest gentlemen you'll ever meet. He'd make an excellent husband. In fact, I fancied him for myself before I married Lord Roderick."

"You did?" Catherine pressed, intrigued. No one had ever told her anything personal about their lives before. She wondered what else Lady Roderick would disclose.

"I did. But I made the mistake of going out on the veranda without a chaperone."

"Oh, I remember! You and Lord Roderick were betrothed that evening."

"Yes. And while I had been hoping to marry Lord Clement, Lord Roderick intended to marry you."

Her cheeks grew warm. "He did?"

She laughed and pressed her fingers to her lips. "But you must never tell him I told you that."

"I don't remember him. Did he and I share a dance?"

"Yes. It was one dance."

"You're happy together, though, aren't you?" Catherine asked.

"Very much so. Despite our shaky beginning, it all worked out. If you think about it, I owe you a favor for letting me marry my husband."

Catherine giggled. "It sounds funny when you put it that way."

"It does, doesn't it? But there are no hard feelings?"

"No, of course not. I don't even remember him."

"I hope you'll let me introduce you to Lord Clement. I think you'll fancy him."

"If he's a friend of yours and Lord Roderick's, then I'm sure I will." Even as Catherine said those words, her pulse raced with unexpected excitement. After two Seasons, maybe things were about to change for the better.

"I'll return as soon as I find him," Lady Roderick promised before she rose to her feet and disappeared into the crowd.

***

Ethan glanced over his shoulder and cringed. Good heavens but Mrs. Duffy and her daughter were a persistent pair! Ever since he walked into the ballroom, the two had sought him out like two hounds hunting a fox. He hurried around a group of gentlemen who were talking and almost ran into the Duke of Rumsey.

"Pardon me, Your Grace," he quickly said.

The duke stiffened but offered him a polite smile. "It's fine, Lord Edon."

"Oh, there you are, you sneaky devil you!" Mrs. Duffy called out from behind him.

Ethan's grimace wasn't lost on the duke whose lips twitched in amusement. "Mrs. and Miss Duffy," he began, peering around Ethan, "I see you are acquainted with Lord Edon."

"Only as an acquaintance at the moment," Mrs. Duffy replied and gave Ethan a wink.

The duke chuckled. "I'll leave you three to talk then."

Ethan scowled at the duke as he left him alone with the two hounds who circled about him. In the past he'd been polite to Lady Catherine, so he thought her father would at least stick around. Well, that only went to prove how little he could count on someone when he needed help.

"Lord Edon, we happened to see you earlier today while we were shopping," the mother said.

"Oh, did you?" Ethan stepped back, not paying attention to where he was going, but knowing he had to back up since the mother and daughter were making it a point to close in on him.

"Yes," the daughter replied, fluffing her blonde curls and batting her eyelashes at him. "You were riding your horse in Hyde Park."

"I thought you said you were shopping," he said.

The mother took another step toward him. "We were, but we thought we'd go to the park to see if you were there."

He stepped back again. "You were looking for me?"

"Well, we wanted to see the notable gentlemen there, and we happened to see you. As soon as we saw you here tonight, I told my daughter that we must talk to you."

He inwardly cringed as he continued to back up. "There are many gentlemen here. As you may have read in the scandalsheets, I'm not exactly suitable for a lady with delicate sensibilities."

"We know better than to believe everything we read."

Her daughter let out a high-pitch laugh that caused him to inwardly shudder. Goodness but there was no way he could bear to listen to that irritating sound for the rest of his life!

"Besides," the mother continued, still creeping toward him, "you're a titled gentleman. You're permitted a few indiscretions."

Oh great. Just his luck. His title was his undoing. If only he could give the blasted thing to his cousin and be done with it!

"Perhaps you and my daughter might partake in a dance?" the mother suggested, slithering closer to him like the Grim Reaper who escorted gentlemen to their eternal abodes before their time.

"Um…well…" He took another step backwards and bumped into someone. Surprised, he turned around and saw Lady Catherine who was sitting in a chair. Inspired, he helped her to her feet and pulled her toward him. "Mrs. and Miss Duffy, I want you to meet Lady Catherine." He lifted her hand and kissed it. "Did you miss me, dearest?" he asked Lady Catherine.

Lady Catherine remained still for a moment before she tried pulling her hand out of his.

He chuckled and squeezed her hand so she couldn't get away from him. "I'm sorry I was gone for so long. I had to discuss the latest happenings," or whatever it was called, "with the Parliament. But I'm back now and can dance with you." Glancing at the mother and daughter, he added, "My intended gets lonely if I leave her for too long. I trust you understand."

"Intended?" The mother's eyes widened as she glanced from Ethan to Lady Catherine. "Forgive me, my lady. If my daughter and I had known…"

"Think nothing of it. We've been keeping it a secret until her father approves," Ethan lied.

17

Before Catherine could protest and give his ploy away, he steered her away from the two ladies and ushered her to the dance floor. Knowing her sense of duty would compel her to dance with him, he waited for the music to start and bowed. She glanced around, let out a frustrated sigh, and curtsied. Good. As he expected, she accepted a dance with him.

"What are you doing?" she muttered under her breath as they began the dance.

"I had to escape from the meddlesome mother and daughter somehow, and you were the only lady I could find who wasn't doing anything." As soon as he said those words, he realized he could have worded it better.

"For your information, I was waiting for someone to return," she replied, a bitter edge underlying her polite tone.

"I apologize, my lady. I didn't mean to imply you don't have any friends."

"Who said I was waiting for a friend? I could've been waiting for a gentleman."

He resisted the urge to laugh. It wasn't that he intended to even think something so rude about her, but it was no secret that Lady Catherine was destined to be a spinster. Sure, she was nice, but no one really knew anything about her, and ladies like that tended to be uninteresting, though he realized it was better than being a lady who was known for questionable activities.

When he didn't reply, she added, "I was waiting for a gentleman, in case you were wondering."

"I'm sure your father will wait for you to return," he replied, mindful to keep his movements in time with the music.

She gasped. "It wasn't my father!"

He glanced at her to see if she was joking, but her face remained serious. "Really?"

"You needn't act surprised," she replied through gritted teeth.

He shrugged. "Actually, I am. I mean, I know you've danced with other gentlemen besides me—"

"One can hardly call you a gentleman," she muttered.

Ignoring her, he continued in a pleasant tone, "Your father does a good job of scouting them out for you."

"He didn't scout you out."

"Oh, he wouldn't. I'm not your type. He has the sense to realize it."

"Thanks…I think."

"I assure you that it's a compliment. I am a rake. Ladies with fine upbringing such as yourself know better than to marry me."

She rolled her eyes. "You sound proud of that."

"I am. Do you know how hard it is to cultivate the rumor? It's not as easy as it seems."

"Somehow I doubt it."

"Well, it's true. And I know there's no danger of your father trying to talk you into marrying me."

"Nor would I choose you, of all gentlemen, to marry."

"And that is also a relief. Your being alone when I needed you most was wonderful timing."

"I *was* waiting for a gentleman."

He chuckled.

"I have a mind to go right over to that mother and daughter and tell them the truth."

She started to leave, so he reached for her arm and stopped her. "I apologize. You were waiting for someone." Maybe there was an uncle or cousin she meant to talk to. That was probably the case. "We should at least finish the dance before we avoid each other for the rest of the night."

Her jaw clenched, she settled down.

"I must admit I'm shocked," he continued. "Usually, you're so docile. You smile, say yes or no, and listen to whatever I ramble on about."

"Perhaps if you said something of interest, I'd be more entertaining."

His eyebrows rose. Who knew Lady Catherine could be so witty? He glanced across the room and saw her father frown at him. Simply for amusement, he grinned at him, knowing it would irk the gentleman to no end. Her father would never come out and tell him to get away from his daughter, but the older gentleman's glowering stares never went unnoticed. And that made Lady Catherine the safest lady he could dance with. Marriage with her was an impossibility.

The music ended, and both breathed a sigh of relief. He bowed. She curtsied. They bolted off in opposite directions, glad to have the horrible dance over with.

Chapter Three

*E*than made it ten steps away from Lady Catherine when his mother ran up to him with a huge smile on her face. "I just heard the good news!" She gave him a hug.

"Mother!" He pushed her away, wondering what she was doing.

"I'm sorry, Ethan, but I was so overcome with joy, I couldn't help myself." Then raising her voice so everyone in the immediate vicinity could hear, she continued, "I can't believe you and Lady Catherine—the Duke of Rumsey's *daughter*—have been secretly engaged this entire time!"

Her words stopped conversations all around them, and Ethan could swear he heard a pin drop somewhere in the room. Refusing to look to the right or left, he focused on his mother and swallowed the lump in his throat. "If you'll join me outside, I'll explain everything."

"What's there to explain?" she asked, again using a high pitch voice that would wake the dead. "You just told Mrs. and Miss Duffy that Lady Catherine's your intended." She clasped her hands together and sighed. "It's so romantic. Just like Romeo and Juliet, except your mother heartily approves of the match. It's time to tell her father, so you and Lady Catherine can finally be together. Even he can't deny true love."

"I wouldn't call it true love, Mother," he protested, heat rising up in his face. Everyone—and that meant every single person in that room—was watching them! Didn't they have anything better to do?

His mother giggled and slipped her arm around his. "Let's talk to her father. Perhaps he and I can work something out. After all, your little secret is out. Everyone knows." She motioned to the stunned expressions on the onlookers' faces.

He felt sick to his stomach. He prayed for the floor to open up and swallow him, but no such relief was going to come. She led him forward. Halfway to the Duke of Rumsey, he dug his heels into the floor and shook his head. "I'm sorry, Mother, but I can't do it. It would break her dear father's heart. The gentleman is insistent she find someone who deserves her."

"You will deserve her. From this moment forward, you will stop doing the dastardly things mentioned in the *Tittletattle*. You will be a respectable gentleman."

She pushed him forward, so now they were within a few feet of the duke. Panicked, he whispered, "I was lying to Mrs. and Miss Duffy to get away from them. Lady Catherine and I hardly know each other."

"Well, we'll resolve that soon enough."

She shoved him again, and he was so stunned that she was still insistent on talking to the duke that he lunged forward and ended up tripping. The world went spinning around him as he toppled to the floor. He was barely aware of the giggles and snickers around him as his mother hovered over him.

"Oh, my poor son," she said in a loud voice, glancing at everyone who turned to look at them. "I keep telling him the Duke of Rumsey is a reasonable gentleman. He'll understand that true love must flourish. His daughter and my son are in love. What could be nobler than that?"

To Ethan's horror, the duke stopped talking to Lord Roderick and looked at Ethan's mother.

"Mother, please," Ethan hissed through his teeth. "You're embarrassing yourself."

She raised an eyebrow in a silent challenge, and with a wide smile, she swirled around to face the duke and curtsied. "Your Grace, I hate to bother you in a middle of such an exquisite ball—one of your finest, might I add—but I just learned of a secret engagement between my son and your daughter." Glancing at Ethan, she motioned for him to stand up.

He shook his head. No way was he going to face the wrath of the Duke of Rumsey!

With an exaggerated sigh, she returned her attention to the duke. "It's a simple thing, Your Grace. Everyone knows about the engagement, so it seems proper to allow the two to finally marry."

The duke's face paled. "Uh…" He scanned the large room where most of the people had stopped talking and dancing to watch them. "Where's my daughter?"

From among the crowd, someone pushed Lady Catherine toward Ethan. She looked horrified. Absolutely and completely horrified. Ethan couldn't blame her. He felt the exact same way. And worse, he was the reason this was happening. Who was to know one simple lie could result in such a catastrophe?

"What's going on here?" her father demanded, looking from Ethan to her.

Lady Catherine gulped. "Nothing."

"Now, now, my lady," his mother began in a soothing tone, "there's no need to worry. My son is one of the wealthiest earls around. He will provide very well for you." Glancing at the Duke of Rumsey, she added, "He can even buy her a separate house if she desires. But—" she wrapped her arm around Lady Catherine's shoulders and urged her over to Ethan—"I don't think it'll come to that. They are deeply in love. Can't you tell just by looking at them?"

Ethan grew dizzy and his vision blurred. A few people chuckled, and Lady Catherine mumbled something about not knowing what any of this was about. But everything was starting to grow dim around him, except for the grave disapproval on the duke's face, which would be forever seared into his memory. He was trapped. His mother was going on and on about the beauty of love, going so far as to quote William Shakespeare. It was too much to take. The room whirled around him, and the next thing he knew, everything went black and he collapsed.

***

As Lord Edon collapsed, Catherine gasped and moved away from him. Everyone stood silent for the longest moment. But no one was more stunned than she was! Just what was Lord Edon's mother thinking in staging this horrific thing?

"Tell me it's not true," her father demanded, looking at her.

"It's not," she blurted out, but not before Lord Edon's mother stepped in front of her, blocking her view of her father.

"It is true. We heard it directly from my son, and I have witnesses. Mrs. and Miss Duffy can testify to it," his mother insisted.

Ignoring Lord Edon's body, the two ladies stepped forward and nodded. "We can," Mrs. Duffy said. "And when he told us Lady Catherine was his intended, Lady Catherine made no protest."

Her father tried to peer around Lord Edon's mother, but she spread her fan out and blocked his view of her. "Your Grace, it is not my place to intrude, but the respectability of my son and your daughter is at stake. Think of how it would look to the Ton if you didn't allow the two to marry."

"I'm sure this is a misunderstanding," he stammered. "I'm sure we can discuss this further in private."

"I don't see how my son's declaration of a secret engagement to Mrs. and Miss Duffy could be a misunderstanding," she replied. "And I happen to know for a fact that Mrs. and Miss Duffy wouldn't lie about such a thing."

The crowd murmured their approval and waited for him to speak.

A prolonged silence filled the room, and Catherine stopped trying to make eye contact with her father. The shame of it all! Who in their right mind would believe she'd be with someone like Lord Edon? A quick scan of the crowd revealed that they not only believed it, but they were enjoying every moment of her humiliation. Her gaze went back to Lord Edon who remained in an unconscious heap on the floor. She had a mind to pour a pitcher of water on him and demand he face this like a gentleman instead of taking the coward's way out.

Lord Edon's mother faced Catherine, clasped her hands in hers, and softly said, "You have nothing to worry about, my lady. I'll see to it my son takes good care of you." Turning to the duke, she continued, "What do you say, Your Grace? Will you give them the opportunity to be together or not?"

Catherine lowered her gaze. If she had to see the disappointment on her father's face, she'd break down and cry. This was the worst thing that could have happened to her. Even a life of spinsterhood would have been more tolerable than the curse of marrying a notorious rake like Lord Edon.

With a resigned sigh, her father muttered, "I give my consent."

From there, the people around them started speaking to one another, and while Catherine felt relief from not being watched anymore, she also became aware of the feeling of dread that grew in the pit of her stomach. She was about to be married to Lord Edon. Her gaze went back to Lord Edon. Resisting the urge to slap him so he'd wake up and see what a mess his lie made, she let out a slight huff and stepped aside so a couple of gentlemen could carry his useless body to another room.

***

The first thing Ethan noticed was the excitement in his mother's voice as she rambled on about the wedding. "It'll be lovely," she gushed. "We'll have it at St. George's Church. I'll put forth the money necessary to make your dress, Catherine. It'll be made of white satin with a striped-gauze overdress and trimmed with Brussels lace. The pearl necklace you're wearing now will be just the thing to go with it."

Ethan groaned and rubbed his forehead. "Mother, stop trying to control what she's going to wear."

From across the room, his mother gasped. "I'm not controlling anything. I figure since this is my doing, I'll pay for the dress and anything else your bride needs."

Bride? He bolted up, but his head spun so he settled back onto the settee in the drawing room and closed his eyes. Goodness gracious, she was talking about *his* bride! For a moment there, he thought she was talking about someone else's wedding, but he recalled the horrifying events and was assured that she was, indeed, talking about *his* wedding.

"Just what I need for a son-in-law," Catherine's father muttered. "He's nothing but a pansy."

At that, Ethan's eyes flew open and he eased into an upright position. "I am *not* a pansy!"

"Of course, you're not, my dear," his mother replied as she hurried over to him and wiped the sweat off his forehead with a handkerchief.

"Mother!" He pushed her hand away. "I can take care of myself." He caught sight of the duke smirking at him and snatched the handkerchief from her when she dabbed his forehead again. "I'm a grown gentleman. Leave me alone."

With a shrug, she returned to her seat, which happened to be next to Catherine's, and sat down. Undaunted by her son's bad mood, she smiled in contentment. "Did I mention how happy I am that Ethan has finally found a good lady to marry?"

"Several times," Catherine's father muttered, rubbing his eyes.

Ethan ventured a look at Catherine who stared at his mother with wide eyes, her face even more pale than usual and her hands clenched together in her lap.

"Forgive me for repeating myself. It's just that I was beginning to give up hope, and now I see that all my fretting has been for nothing. What a relief!" Catherine, her father, and Ethan grumbled, but she pressed on as if she hadn't heard them. "I want this to be your special day, Catherine, so tell me what I can do to make your fairytale wedding come true."

Catherine glanced at her father who looked heavenward, sighed, and shook his head. "Uh…well…"

Ethan knew exactly what they were thinking. They wanted out of the wedding just as badly as he did. "This is nonsense, Mother. You know very well I didn't have a secret engagement with…with," he motioned to Catherine, "her."

Catherine glared at him. "Her?"

Her father, just as quick to respond, snapped, "Lady Catherine is how you will refer to her."

"Now, now… Let's not be hasty," his mother replied, still using the cheerful tone that was grating on his nerves. "This benefits everyone in this room. Catherine will live very well off my son's assets. He's amassed a surprising fortune over the years."

"Through gambling," the duke muttered.

"He won't do that anymore." She shot Ethan a pointed look. "Right, Ethan?"

He sighed. "I'm a grown gentleman, Mother." Why did he have to keep saying it? And seriously, it wasn't like he enjoyed it.

He only wanted to lose his fortune, but for the life of him, he couldn't lose a hand. He came close once, but at the last minute, the other gentleman quit and left him with more money. How was he supposed to deal with that? Why was he gambling? Obviously, it was only getting him into more trouble because it made him more attractive to the ladies. "I will give it up." Before his mother could take credit for his change of heart, he added, "And not because you said to do it, Mother. I've never lost a game. Something is wrong with me. I can't lose to save my life."

"Because you cheat?" her father guessed.

Ethan's jaw dropped. "I'd never cheat. I have my honor to protect."

He rolled his eyes. "Such as it is."

"There you go, Catherine. My son is done with his gambling. All his money will be yours to enjoy. Considering he's one of the wealthiest gentlemen at this ball tonight, you'll do very well with this marriage. As for Ethan, he'll do well to settle down with a nice, respectable lady, and few ladies are as nice and respectable as you. This is an excellent match. Even better, your son will have a title to his name when Ethan dies."

Catherine placed her hand over her stomach, looking as if she was going to lose her dinner. As a respectable lady, any thoughts to lovemaking would make her queasy to her stomach. The only thing he knew about the act was that the quicker it was done, the better. Wives were for the duty to a gentleman's lineage. Mistresses were for pleasure. And quite frankly, Ethan had no desire for either. Why couldn't his mother understand and appreciate the fact that he was meant to enjoy a life in the country removed from all this nonsense? He let out a weary sigh and put his head in his hands. All hopes for a peaceful life evaporated right before his eyes.

"Your Grace," his mother began, "do I have your permission to tell your daughter about her duty in the bedroom?"

Appalled by his mother's brazen question, Ethan stood up. "You continually worry about what the Ton thinks of me, and yet you have the audacity to ask something so personal to a duke in his own home?"

His mother shrugged. "I doubt His Grace knows how to handle this matter." Glancing at Catherine, she added, "It's a delicate thing, and gentlemen aren't very good with those types of discussions."

"Why do you persist in embarrassing me?" he demanded.

"Me embarrass you?" She rose to her feet and squared her shoulders back. "I have to find out about your indiscretions through the *Tittletattle*."

The duke rose to his feet. "We don't need to hear anymore." He hurried over to Catherine, took her by the elbow, and helped her stand up. "We agreed that the marriage will take place in a month. The Banns will be read over the next three Sundays, and after that," he gulped, "the ceremony will take place." Turning his attention to Ethan's mother, he continued, "In the meantime, your son has no need to get near my daughter."

His mother nodded. When the duke opened the door and left with Catherine, his mother waited until they were out of earshot to clap her hands. "How exciting! That went better than I hoped."

"I don't understand you, Mother. They're miserable about this."

She waved her hand in a dismissive manner. "They're in shock. It's bound to happen considering everything they've been through. Look who she's marrying." She motioned to him. "But what other choice did she have? Spinsterhood? That's a terrible fate for a duke's daughter. Now he knows his daughter's future is secure. Plus, his grandson will be an earl. It'll be a good consolation when he's on his deathbed." She paused and studied him. "You will do everything you can to make sure he gets that grandson, won't you?"

"You really need to ask?" he replied, both appalled and irritated that she needed to pose such a question to a gentleman who had a reputation as a rake.

"Oh, you're right. You've been with lots of ladies…and not-so-ladylike ladies. If anyone can give Catherine a son, it's you. I just hope you remember to do your duty to her instead of running off to seek pleasure elsewhere. Remember, you have an obligation to the crown."

He stared at her as she skipped out of the room and shook his head. His mother, who had the nerve to refer to herself as a lady, had the tendency to be as blunt as a gentleman at the gambling tables.

"What kind of a travesty did I get myself into?" he mumbled, and deciding he'd had enough excitement for one night, he slipped out the window.

Chapter Four

"You have a request from someone who wants to visit you," Opal told Catherine who was softly crying into her handkerchief.

Catherine didn't stir from her daybed. She swallowed the lump in her throat. What if the request came from Lord Edon or his mother? Taking a deep breath, she ventured, "Who is it?"

"Lady Roderick."

She wiped the tears from her eyes and sat up. "Lady Roderick?"

"Yes. Would you like her to come for a visit?"

After she nodded, Opal left her bedchamber. Catherine wondered what Lady Roderick wanted to talk about. She hadn't visited her before. The only time she'd talked to Lady Roderick was whenever she saw her at balls, and their conversations were always brief.

She recalled their conversation the previous evening when Lady Roderick wanted to introduce her to Lord Clement. Maybe that's what she wanted to talk about. But didn't she know about Catherine's sudden betrothal? Catherine thought back to what transpired after her father had arranged the wedding with Lord Edon's mother. Most of it was a blur. She didn't remember seeing Lady Roderick after her father escorted her back to the ball. People expressed their congratulations on the upcoming wedding, but Lady Roderick hadn't been one of them. So maybe she didn't see the events that transpired and the resulting wedding announcement.

Catherine grimaced. Why anyone would congratulate her on her upcoming wedding to Lord Edon was beyond her. They probably said it to be polite. She put her hand over her stomach. She was going to be sick if she kept thinking about it.

Opal returned and offered her a smile. "I sent word for you, my lady. Lady Roderick should be here soon. What dress would you like to wear?"

Relieved to occupy her thoughts with something other than her upcoming marriage, Catherine rose from her daybed and selected a green dress to wear.

As Opal helped her out of her morning dress, she said, "Sometimes a change of dress can raise a lady's spirit."

"It's going to take more than changing dresses to make me feel better." Realizing she spoke aloud, she quickly added, "Forgive me. I shouldn't be complaining. Yesterday, I moped because I had no suitor, and today, I mope because I'm to be married." She shrugged. "I'm not happy, no matter what happens, am I?"

"No one can blame you for being upset that you're marrying someone your father doesn't approve of."

"Lord Edon and I never had a secret engagement. He made that up to avoid being chased by an eager young lady."

"I didn't think there was a secret engagement. I might not know the details on how your betrothal came about, but I know you well enough to understand Lord Edon manipulated the situation to his advantage."

Catherine raised her arms while her maid slipped the green dress over her head. "Well, he might have come up with the lie, but it was his mother who forced the issue."

"She didn't!"

She let out a heavy sigh. "She's quite excited about the marriage, too. I'm not sure how she managed it, but with her insistence that Lord Edon and I were in love, my father couldn't say no to a marriage in front of everyone. He was trapped into agreeing to it."

"Perhaps your marriage won't be as bad as you fear," she replied as she buttoned the back of her dress.

"Lord Edon's a rake. Of all the gentlemen I could be marrying, it has to be him? He's not even a decent rake."

Opal giggled. "I wasn't aware that there was a decent type of rake."

"No, I suppose not. But Lord Edon doesn't even try to hide his indiscretions. I haven't read the *Tittletattle*, but I hear he's in it more than anyone else. Sometimes I wonder if he wants to be featured so he has something to brag about."

Opal finished with the dress and motioned to the vanity. Catherine sat in the chair and watched as she styled her hair. Thankfully, she had the comfort of knowing Opal would be with her after she married Lord Edon. Once Opal finished, she handed her a hand mirror so Catherine could inspect the back of her hair.

"You did a lovely job," Catherine said. "You always do a lovely job." Too bad she wasn't lovely enough to do justice to her hairstyle or dress.

Pushing aside her thoughts, she left her bedchamber and went down the stairs. Since Lady Roderick hadn't arrived yet, she traveled the hallway until she found her father in his fencing room. She waited until he turned to her, lowered his smallsword, and took off his mask.

"What is it, Cathy?"

She stepped into the room and studied her fingernails. "Lady Roderick is coming by for a visit, and I didn't know what to do until she arrived so I came to see what you're doing."

"Oh, I'm just thinking of what I'll say to Lord Edon when I invite him over."

"You're going to invite him here?" She shouldn't have been surprised since she was going to marry him, but he was the last person she expected her father to willingly talk to.

"I want to make sure he treats you like the lady you are. Given his reputation, I think some incentive to behave himself when you're around is only suitable."

"I wish he'd found someone else to dance with when he was trying to get rid of Mrs. and Miss Duffy," she replied. "If he had, then his mother would have found someone else to pawn him off on. His mother must be desperate to find him a wife."

"How fortunate for us she found you when she did," he muttered. "As much as I'd like to change the circumstances, I can't. Lord Edon doesn't deserve you."

Well, there was no denying that.

"It makes me sick to see you with him, but short of a duel, there's nothing else I can do."

She gasped. "You won't challenge him to a duel?"

"No. Unfortunately, it's been outlawed, and I'm not the kind of gentleman who breaks the law. Unlike Lord Edon, I believe in behaving honorably."

"I suspect that's what his mother was betting on."

His hold tightened on his mask. "I know she was, which is why she gave that grand display in front of everyone." He closed his eyes and gritted his teeth. "Apparently, it was my undoing to leave your side."

"You can't be with me all the time."

"While that's nice of you to say, I failed you."

She walked over to him and embraced him. "You didn't fail me."

He wrapped his arms around her and sighed. "I just want the best for you, and God knows Lord Edon isn't it."

"I know, but there's no going back in time and undoing what's been done."

He released her and smiled. "You're a brave young lady."

"Courage has nothing to do with it. I just know that I have no other option."

"I'm going to do everything I can to make sure Lord Edon treats you with the respect you deserve. I won't have him making a fool of you."

The butler entered the room. "Lady Roderick is here, Lady Catherine."

Her father patted her on the arms. "Have a good visit with your friend."

"She's not my friend. I hardly know her," Catherine replied.

"Maybe this is the beginning of a friendship. Given your upcoming marriage, you could use a friend or two to help you cope with Lord Edon."

"With any luck, I'll be able to live in my own home like his mother suggested."

"That would be best."

She turned to the butler and followed him down the hallway until she reached the drawing room where Lady Roderick sat on a settee. "Will you bring us some tea?" Catherine asked the butler.

He nodded and bowed before he left the room.

Up to this point, Catherine had been so focused on her impending marriage that she hadn't given full thought to what Lady Roderick's visit meant. She couldn't recall the last time she was paid a social call. Sure, she had ladies visit in order to get into the good graces of her father, but Lady Roderick was here because she wanted to actually spend time with her. And that made Catherine nervous since she'd never talked to anyone who simply wanted to get to know her.

Offering a tentative smile, she sat across from her. "How are you?"

"I'm doing well," Lady Roderick replied.

"If I recall right, you have a son?"

"Yes. Perry will be one next month."

"That's wonderful. Your husband must be happy."

"He is. We named our son after his childhood friend, Lord Clement. He's the one I had hoped to introduce you to last night."

As the butler came into the room and set the tray of tea and biscuits on the table, Catherine nodded. "I remember, and I was waiting for him when Lord Edon whisked me away to dance with him. He only did it to dissuade Mrs. and Miss Duffy from coming after him, and then he made up a horrible lie that he and I were sharing a secret engagement." Even thinking about it brought tears to her eyes. She didn't know if she was angry or depressed over the recent events. "I'm sorry." She dabbed the tears from her eyes. "I can't seem to stop crying over the misfortunate events that transpired shortly after I danced with him."

Lady Roderick retrieved a handkerchief from her reticule and handed it to her. "I heard. Lord Clement understands the situation."

Catherine held onto the handkerchief and shook her head. "I don't know how it happened. One minute, I was waiting for you, then I'm off dancing, and before I know it, Lord Edon's mother is telling everyone I'm engaged to her son. It was the most humiliating thing that's ever happened to me. Of all gentlemen I might entertain a secret engagement with, Lord Edon is the last one I'd pick."

"I don't think anyone believes his mother. She's desperate to see him married to a reputable lady."

She shivered. "I hate to think of all his wicked activities."

"Try not to think about it." Before Catherine replied, she added, "I know that's easier said than done."

Catherine wiped more tears from her eyes and forced herself to laugh in hopes of lightening the mood. "I'm a terrible hostess." She placed the handkerchief next to her on the chair and reached for the teapot.

"You have a lot on your mind."

"Even so, I can pour a cup of tea." Or at least, that was what she thought before she lost her hold on the cup she was filling. The cup fell onto the rug and the tea spilled out of it. "Oh, dear me!" She retrieved a folded up napkin and got on her knees so she could use it to soak up the spill.

Lady Roderick hurried over to her and wrapped her arm around her shoulders. "The maid can clean it up."

She was right. Catherine stood up, clasping her trembling hands so she wouldn't do anything else to look stupid. "I don't know what's wrong with me. I'm not usually this clumsy."

"It's nerves. You've been through a lot in the past day. Why don't you sit down and I'll notify the maid?"

Figuring how nervous she was, Catherine decided that was the best thing to do. She sat in her chair and picked up the handkerchief, which she twirled around her fingers. As Lady Roderick left the drawing room, Catherine stared at the spill on the rug and wondered what was wrong with her. No wonder she didn't have any friends. She lacked sufficient social graces. If her father hadn't been a duke, no one would bother talking to her.

Lady Roderick returned with one of the maids and smiled at Catherine. "Please don't worry about the spill. We all drop things every now and then."

Though she was still embarrassed, she smiled. "That's very kind of you to say."

"There's nothing kind about it," she replied as the maid placed a new cup on the tray before she cleaned up the mess. "Do you mind if I pour the tea?"

"No. Please do." Glancing at the maid, she said, "Thank you."

"Think nothing of it, my lady," the maid told her then left the room, carrying the discarded cup and cleaning bowl with her.

"I once spilled wine all over Lady Montgomery's dress at a dinner party."

Catherine wasn't sure if she was telling her the truth, but even if she wasn't, her intent was sweet. Relaxing, she accepted the cup Lady Roderick handed her.

"I came because I wanted to apologize for not bringing Lord Clement to meet you sooner. If I had, you wouldn't be engaged to Lord Edon. My sister wanted to speak to me, so I was delayed in talking to him. By the time, I did find him, Lord Edon's mother was making a fuss about the engagement."

"You couldn't have known she was going to do that."

"I know, but I had horrible timing."

"It's all right, Lady Roderick. I appreciate the fact that you wanted to introduce me to your friend."

She finished drinking some tea and said, "I hope you'll call me Claire. I enjoy talking to you and hope we can be friends."

Pleased, she smiled. "I'd like that. And you can call me Catherine."

"I was planning on visiting the linen-draper to select material for a new dress. Would you like to join me?"

Catherine couldn't recall the last time a lady invited her to go shopping with her, and despite her apprehension that she might say or do something to embarrass herself, she agreed. She suspected Claire would accept her, faults and all. And it would be nice to have a friend to go shopping with. Once they were done with the tea and biscuits, they headed out for a day of shopping.

Chapter Five

"*A*nd to think no one thought you could be conquered," Mr. Christopher Robinson teased.

Ethan lifted his head from the table in the corner of the room at White's. Coming here was probably a bad idea, but he didn't know where else to go. His mother wouldn't leave him alone at the townhouse, and he didn't want to risk running into Catherine or her father. Fortunately, her father wasn't a member of White's, so this was the safest place he could be.

With a sigh, he directed his attention to his friend. "Enjoying my misery?"

Christopher shrugged and sat across from him. "Marriage isn't the worst thing that can happen to you."

"The Duke of Rumsey's going to be my father-in-law."

He chuckled. "You have my sympathies. I thought Lord Roderick was unbearable, but I admit His Grace is worse."

"Cleaning out Lord Roderick's stalls is nothing compared to marrying the duke's daughter. At least Lord Roderick showed some mercy."

"Mercy? He made me empty and clean chamber pots!"

Despite himself, he chuckled. "He didn't."

"He did. It was the most humiliating summer of my life."

"Whatever did you do to deserve such a thing?"

"I tried to help his poor wife escape the prison he trapped her in, but he found out and made me a chamber maid. As it turned out, his wife ended up wanting to be with him. Who knew?"

Despite his bad mood, Ethan found himself chuckling. "Those two are happy together." Anyone could tell that just by watching them.

"It wasn't always so."

"Well, Lord Roderick doesn't have a meddling mother and irate father-in-law to deal with. I got an invite to the Duke of Rumsey's townhouse. I hope he remembers that dueling isn't legal anymore. Though I admit, a duel is better than cleaning chamber pots."

"You'd think so until you had to clean them."

Ethan rolled his eyes, sure he was exaggerating.

Christopher pulled up a chair and sat next to him. "So why are you moping over here instead of robbing gentlemen at the gambling table out of spite?"

"I'm not gambling anymore."

"What?"

"I can't lose. I'm like poor King Midas. Everything I touch turns to gold."

Christopher chuckled. "Oh, to have such a problem as that!"

"It's dreadful. I've amassed a great fortune, and it's that fortune that got me in trouble. If I wasn't as wealthy as I am, mothers wouldn't have been hounding me to marry their daughters. They were no better than a bunch of vultures circling a dying prey." He shuddered.

"Now you're rambling on like a lunatic."

"It's not fair. All I want to do is spend my time alone in a secluded manor and read books. I was hoping my mother would come to her senses at some point, but she trapped me into a marriage. I'll never have peace and quiet again. My life is about to be filled with countless trips to balls, the theatre, stores, and lots of other social endeavors."

He smirked. "Yes, your life is about to become very distressing."

"I can't help but notice you're enjoying my agony."

Christopher burst out laughing. "Is it really that bad? You do all those things now. Except you'll have a wife. Wives don't get in the way. You can live your life; she can live hers. Not every wife has to live with her husband. My mother didn't live with my father. Then he died, and she went shortly afterwards. After that, I was my cousin's ward."

"You don't understand. My mother is going to befriend my wife, and the two will conspire against me. My life won't be my own."

"Is it your own now?"

Ethan wanted to chastise Christopher for making the disheartening observation, but he couldn't deny it. His mother kept pestering him, nudging him not-too-gently to balls to meet suitable young ladies. Her ploy worked. Next, he'd undoubtedly be victim to his mother's plans to make a love match between him and Catherine.

She wanted more than for him to get a wife so he could have an heir. What she most wanted was for him to be as happily married as she'd been with his father. Theirs hadn't been a love match in the beginning, but over time, they realized they loved each other. He'd once thought she was exaggerating the depth of their love for each other, but when his father died, he understood how wrong he'd been.

And now she was going to make it her life's work to secure the same fate for him. He couldn't begrudge her for her desire. She meant well, but the lady needed to understand that a love match was rare and with someone as boring as Catherine, he didn't see how it was possible.

Christopher motioned to a room where gentlemen were playing cards. "Come with me. I want to win a few hands."

"I told you I'm not gambling anymore," Ethan protested.

"Who said anything about you gambling? I want you to come along and teach me your tricks."

"I don't have any tricks."

"Then sit with me for good luck. Maybe some of your fortune will rub off on me."

With a heavy sigh, Ethan figured it was better to be distracted by the games than mope over things he couldn't change. He rose to his feet and walked with Christopher to the other room.

***

"You want me to fence?" Ethan slowly asked, not sure he heard right.

When Catherine's father told him he wanted to speak with him, he assumed they'd go to his library where he'd give him a lecture on how to treat his daughter. He didn't expect him to engage in a sport.

"Are you familiar with fencing?"

"I've done it a few times." He didn't enjoy it, but he knew better than to say no to the Duke of Rumsey.

"There's a room where you may change into the appropriate clothing. My valet will tend to anything you require." He motioned to the small room.

Ethan glanced around the large fencing room and wondered if His Grace did this often or once in a while. Deciding it would be better if he didn't ask, he settled for going to the small room where, sure enough, the valet was waiting. To say changing clothes was awkward would be an understatement. The whole thing was unbelievably nerve-wracking. In some ways, it was worse than if His Grace had went on a screaming rampage. Just what was he supposed to talk about while he was fencing with him?

When Ethan was in the fencing clothes, he returned to Catherine's father who was wiping down the smallswords. Since her father's back was turned to him, Ethan cleared his throat so he'd know he was ready. For a moment, her father gave no indication that he heard him. He just kept on cleaning the blades, a process that was beginning to worry Ethan. Was it his imagination or was her father enjoying those blades a little too much?

In one swift motion, her father spun around, and Ethan couldn't help but notice that the smallswords were pointed at his nose. Ethan narrowed his eyes and saw how sharp the ends were. All right. So maybe this wasn't merely a sport. Maybe His Grace had a nefarious reason for inviting him over for a game of fencing.

Her father lowered the smallswords and handed one to Ethan. "You'll find your mask over there."

As much as Ethan wanted to go right back to the small room, change into his clothes and hurry out of the townhouse, he knew he had to stay there and play the game her father wanted. Swallowing the lump in his throat, he went to the bench and picked up the mask. With a glance at the other gentleman who was putting his mask on, he followed suit and did the same. He took a deep breath, assured that there wasn't anything His Grace had put in the mask to suffocate him. Sure, her father didn't strike him as the type to murder someone, but desperate men did desperate things. Maybe this was the very thing that would make him do the unthinkable.

Gripping the smallsword in his hand, Ethan ventured, "Your Grace, I don't mean to put a damper on what's about to transpire, but I just want to say I'm relieved they now forbid duels."

Her father paused and after a long moment of silence, he said, "I don't recall mentioning a duel. Did I mention a duel, Lord Edon?"

Gulping, he shook his head. "No."

"I think it's odd that you mention it."

"Oh, well, I," he cleared his throat, "I was making conversation." He let out a weak laugh. "Just for something to say. That's all."

"Hmm... In that case, I think it's a shame that someone can't sign a young gentleman up to be a soldier so he can stop Napoleon."

"I understand." Ethan knew that was exactly what her father would do if he could.

Her father moved to the center of the room and lifted his smallsword. "Are you ready?"

Ethan had the feeling that her father wasn't going to make the game easy on him, and he was right. His Grace was an expert fencer, and he made no hesitation of showing off his skills. Ethan had to struggle to keep up with his fast pace. A few times he slipped and almost got jabbed by the smallsword. He managed to recover from his blunders and thought he was doing well in holding his own until it occurred to him that her father was purposely letting him think he was an adequate competitor. As much as Ethan tried to take an offensive stance, he only found himself stuck taking defensive measures.

"There may be a law against duels, as you pointed out, but I'm afraid accidents happen while fencing, despite the protective gear," His Grace said, barely out of breath.

Gasping for air, Ethan managed to ask, "But there are no defects in your fencing clothing, are there?"

"I hope not."

He made a move to strike his chest, but Ethan managed to block his smallsword.

"I brought up Catherine to be a lady," the Duke said, taking another offensive maneuver which Ethan barely stopped.

"I'm aware of that, Your Grace."

"Are you?" He stepped forward and lunged at him.

"Yes." Ethan stumbled in an effort to avoid him and ended up falling on his back.

Her father pointed his smallsword at the base of Ethan's throat before he could get up. "I don't know what kind of perversions you're used to, and quite frankly, I don't want to know. But we're going to get one thing clear. You'll be gentle with my daughter. That means in and out of bed. I can't stop you from doing the disgusting things you do when you're not with her, but I require you to be discrete. If I catch one more item of gossip about you in the *Tittletattle*, you'll answer to me. If you so much as treat my daughter the way you treat one of your whores, I'll make you wish you'd never been born. From this moment forward, you will be a gentleman in every sense of the word. Do you understand?"

Gulping, Ethan nodded, praying that this whole ordeal was over.

The duke removed the smallsword from his throat and motioned for him to stand up. "This game is over. You may rise to your feet like a gentleman."

After a moment's hesitation, he obeyed, making sure there was enough distance between them so he wouldn't be on the receiving end of the smallsword again.

"I'll let you change back into your clothes, but don't forget that I'm watching everything you're doing."

Ethan headed toward the small room where the valet waited to help him change clothes, and as much as he struggled to keep a casual pace, he found himself hurrying for the door. By the time he was out of the duke's viewing range, he breathed a sigh of relief and removed his mask. He wiped the sweat from his forehead, convinced that some of the perspiration was a result of the duke's words.

"What a terrible thing it is to fall under the wrath of a protective father," he mumbled as he rushed through the process of removing the fencing gear.

"I'm sorry, my lord. Did you say something?" the valet asked.

He shook his head. "Not of any consequence." What did any of it matter? He was doomed no matter what he did. Between his mother and his father-in-law, his only means of escape was death. And given his young age and health, he feared death was a long ways off.

Chapter Six

*E*than entered through the servants' stairs of Agatha's townhouse late that evening. Once he made sure the hallway leading to the library was clear, he hurried down it. Without knocking, he opened the door and slipped into the room.

Agatha glanced up from her desk where she was writing and gasped.

He quickly lowered the hood of his cloak and pressed his fingers to his lips. "It's all right. It's just me."

Pressing a hand to her heart, she took a deep breath and released it. "You're horrible, Ethan. What are you doing here?" she hissed in a low voice.

"I need to ask you a favor."

"I can't put another falsehood about you into the *Tittletattle* so soon. Even you aren't so notorious that you have to grace the pages of every edition that gets published."

"I'm not here to get another mention in the *Tittletattle*."

With a sigh of relief, she said, "Good."

He walked over to her desk and sat in the chair across from her. "Actually, I came here to ask if you'd not mention how poor I am."

"But you insisted on it."

"I know." He groaned and ran his fingers through his hair. "It seemed like such a good idea at the time."

"It was. I think it'll get those horrible mothers to relent and finally stop trying to pair you up with their daughters. Second to a title, ladies crave money. And who can blame them? Shopping is a very pleasant experience."

"But you have to stop it from getting into the scandalsheets, Agatha!"

Her eyes grew wide and she shushed him. "If anyone finds out you just snuck into my townhouse, we'll be accused of creating a scandal."

Lowering his voice, he said, "I'm sorry. You're right. And right now, a scandal is the worst thing that can happen to me." Really, it was. He could see the Duke of Rumsey's face clearly in his mind. The gentleman would narrow those cold beady eyes at him and frown as if he was asked to clean chamber pots. The image alone was enough to make him sick to his stomach. "I have to be careful. I can't do anything to upset my father-in-law."

"Your father-in-law? I didn't hear you were married."

"Not yet. The wedding will be in three weeks, four days, fourteen hours and thirty-six seconds." When her eyebrows rose in surprise, he added, "Not that I'm keeping track of the passage of time or anything."

"When did the engagement happen?"

"That night I went to the Duke of Rumsey's ball."

"The same night you came here begging me to put that juicy bit of information about you in the *Tittletattle*?"

He nodded and clutched his stomach. "Yes. It was the worst night of my life."

She burst out laughing but quickly placed her hand over her mouth to quiet herself.

"It's not funny."

She giggled. "For you, it's not. For me, it's hilarious."

He rolled his eyes. "I should have expected such an uncaring response from a lady who writes gothic horror under a gentleman's name." After a moment's pause, he added, "I'm shocked you haven't heard."

"I've been writing. I'm almost done with this story. Then you can hand it to the publisher at Minerva Press."

"Do you take delight in pretending to be a gentleman all the time?"

"I do it because I don't want anyone who reads my work to know I'm a lady."

"I find it hard to believe you can pull off so many identities," Ethan commented.

She shrugged. "I only have two. Gerard Addison contributes to the *Tittletattle*, and Gilbert Horlock writes gothic horror. It's easy to keep track of them."

"Even so, I think you'll slip at some point and expose one of them."

"You don't give me enough credit, Ethan. I'm mindful to watch what I'm doing."

"Maybe." He couldn't manage it if it was him. Turning his attention back to her, he pressed, "You'll forget the item I asked you to write about me being poor, won't you?"

"I wish I could, but I can't."

Stiffening in his seat, he asked, "What?"

With an apologetic smile, she shrugged. "I submitted it yesterday morning."

"But why?"

"Because you asked me to. You were rather insistent it happen right away, so I didn't delay."

He threw back his head and groaned, gripping the arms of the chair so he wouldn't scream. This couldn't be happening to him. Of all the times Agatha was prompt about submitting something to the *Tittletattle*, it had to be this one time when the duke would kill him if he heard of it!

"I'm sorry, Ethan."

He got the image of Catherine's father in his mind. The gentleman stood over him, a smallsword pressed against his throat, and this time, he had no mask to protect him.

Agatha rose from her chair and hurried over to him. Giving his face a gentle pat, she asked, "Are you all right?"

"My life is over. The duke is going to make me participate in a duel."

"Oh, don't be hysterical. Duels are against the law."

He shook his head and tried not to cry. "You don't know the power of his fury. He'll cut me in half and feed me to the dogs." Glancing at her, he added, "I'm too young to die."

She sighed in exasperation and crossed her arms. "You're being absurd."

"You didn't see the way he glared at me while we were fencing today. He hates me."

"Just because he harbors feelings of ill will toward you, it doesn't mean he hates you."

Ethan lessened his hold on the arms of the chair and wiped his forehead. He was sweating again. This wasn't good. His hands started to shake and he had to clasp them to stop the shaking from getting out of control. "He does hate me. I'm a vile gentleman who is about to ruin his daughter. He wants my head on a silver platter."

"And to think I'm the one who writes gothic horror instead of you," Agatha muttered with an exasperated look on her face. "I demand you pull yourself together at once. When the item comes out on the *Tittletattle*, you will look the Duke of Rumsey in the eye and tell him it's not true. Ethan, you know better than anyone that you can't believe everything you read in the *Tittletattle*."

"You don't understand him."

"And you do?"

"Yes. I was fencing with him today, and he made it clear that I'm supposed to have a spotless reputation from now on."

"You'll be fine. You have more money than most titled gentlemen. Have your steward talk to him. Show him your books. I wouldn't be surprised if you are wealthier than him."

He shrugged. Whether he had more money than the duke was irrelevant. The gentleman was going to be furious he was mentioned in the *Tittletattle*, especially since he just warned him about it. Slapping his hands on the armchairs, he let out a weary sigh. He rose to his feet and pulled the hood of his cloak over his head. "If I mysteriously disappear, you know the duke killed me."

Though she didn't respond, he could tell she thought he was exaggerating. Well, maybe if she had a smallsword pressed to her throat, she'd be more understanding.

"You have no need to fret. I'll make sure no one sees me," he softly said as he crossed the room so he could reach the door.

"You'll be fine," she assured him.

"I know I'll be fine getting out of here, but who knows how things will go when that tidbit about me shows up in the *Tittletattle*."

"Ethan!" she hissed.

Before she could criticize him further, he slipped out of the library and scurried down the hall until he found the servants' stairs. In no time at all, he was back on the street, safe from discovery. If only it was so easy to avoid Catherine's father.

***

To Ethan's further dismay, it wasn't the Duke of Rumsey who first found out about the *Tittletattle's* contents. He had just finished praying for absolution from all his sins in case he was about to step into eternity, because of an ill-fated smallsword, when his mother tracked him down in the hallway.

"What is this about you being a pauper?" she demanded, practically shoving a copy of the gossip paper into his arms.

He reluctantly took it and scanned through it until he came across "Gerard Addison's" submission. *Though Lord Edon might dress the part of a dandy, it's only on the surface. If it weren't for kin buying him clothes, he'd be exposed for the pauper he really is.*

"You've been telling people you're as poor as a church mouse?" his mother asked, her hands on her hips.

Glancing around the hallway to make sure none of the servants heard her, he was relieved to see no one in sight. He took her by the elbow and led her to the library, which was the nearest room. Once he closed the door to ensure their privacy, he turned to her. "I'm appalled you'd believe anything in a gossip paper." Then, as if he couldn't care less what was in the *Tittletattle*, he tossed it on the desk and went to the chair across the room.

Undaunted by his deliberate show of indifference, she followed him, gritting her teeth. "You will not ruin this for me, Ethan. The Banns have been read once already. The other two times will occur, and then there will be a wedding."

"I didn't tell anyone I was poor." It wasn't a direct lie since, technically, it was Agatha who did it. "Besides, who is going to believe such an outrageous thing? Look around you. I own this townhouse."

"No. Your father owned it. You inherited it."

"And we're still living in it. You needed a new carriage last month, and I got you one. Our family crest is engraved in gold. Could I do that if I was poor?"

"You gamble so much. One of these days, you're bound to lose everything."

"No, I won't. I've given up gambling, remember?" He gave her a pointed look. "You insisted on it the night you arranged my engagement."

"But how do I know you won't do it anyway?"

Because the Duke of Rumsey wasn't shy when it came to showing off his skills with a smallsword, he thought. But he didn't dare tell her that. Instead, he pressed his hand to his chest and gave her a wounded look. "I can't believe what I'm hearing. I gave you my word."

"You're a rake. Breaking your word is what you do best."

"But not to my mother. Seriously? Have I been such a horrible son that you think I wouldn't honor my word to you?"

She shook her head. "Don't play innocent with me. You've been promising me you'd try to find a nice, respectable lady to marry, but I've had to watch you go through each Season without an engagement."

"I never gave my word on that. You insisted and assumed I went along with it."

She gasped. "You can't turn this around so it looks like I'm in error."

"I kept telling you I wanted to hand over my title to my cousin, but you wouldn't hear of it. I never made a pretense of wanting to marry a lady and pass on my title to an heir."

He knew he should have enjoyed the moment when she realized he was right, but he couldn't when he saw her countenance fall. With a sigh, he stood up and hugged her. "I know you mean well, Mother."

"A gentleman can't be happy unless he has a good lady by his side," she replied.

"I do." He pulled away from her and grinned. "I have you."

Though she shook her head, a slight smile graced her lips. "You know I meant a wife. Your father said he fared far better with me in his life. He was happy."

"I know he was."

"I want you to be happy, too."

Deciding not to insist that a gentleman could be happy living in the country and spending his days reading books, he allowed her to have the final word on the matter. It wouldn't change anything. He was still going to marry Catherine, as long as her father let him live.

"If you believed I was a pauper, I suppose the Duke of Rumsey will, too." And he needed to go over to his townhouse to assure the gentleman that it wasn't true.

"I doubt the duke resorts to reading the *Tittletattle*. He's a refined gentleman."

"He does because he wants to know who will make a suitable husband for his daughter. Or rather, who won't make a suitable husband."

She patted his arm and smiled. "But you *will* make a suitable husband."

"No, I won't, and you've just confined a poor young lady to a life with me."

"You're a suitable gentleman, Ethan. You've always taken good care of me, and because you take care of me, I expect you'll do the same for your wife."

"You only see what you want to see," he replied. "All right. I must make arrangements to see the duke."

"Say no more. I'll leave you alone."

After she left the room, he turned his attention to what he'd say when he confronted Catherine's father.

Chapter Seven

The Duke of Rumsey's eyes bore into Ethan, and though sweat trickled down his back, Ethan refused to break eye contact. The duke remained sitting behind his desk, and since he hadn't offered Ethan a seat, Ethan stood across from him. But Ethan wouldn't yield and run from the library. If he was going to be dealing with the duke for the rest of his life, he needed to pretend the duke couldn't intimidate him. And considering the weight of the duke's stare, that was no easy feat.

"How did news of your impoverished status make it into the *Tittletattle*?" the duke asked.

Ethan shrugged. "How does anything make it into the *Tittletattle*?"

"Do you think by answering my question with a question that you're being clever?"

"No, Your Grace."

"Are you telling me that the *Tittletattle* makes up stories about you?"

Ethan paused because this was a trick question. If he said yes, he'd expose himself and Agatha. If he said no, he'd admit he was poor. "Quite frankly, I don't think the *Tittletattle* should exist. All it does is create problems." There. That should throw him off the trail.

"You didn't answer me."

Ethan inwardly groaned. Why couldn't the gentleman forget the blasted question?

"I want to see your steward," the duke finally said.

"No."

"No?"

"No!" Ethan took a deep breath and strengthened his resolve. "Either you believe me or you don't, but I already told you the truth. I am not a pauper."

The duke didn't blink, and though it took all of Ethan's willpower, he didn't either. The duke clenched and unclenched his jaw a couple of times before he finally spoke. "This is how it's going to be? I'm going to ask you questions, and you're going to be disrespectful enough to either ignore me or refuse my request?"

"With all due respect, you didn't request to see my steward. You *demanded* to see him."

He tightened his hold on his armchair. "And if I had asked?"

"I'd still say no."

He closed his eyes. Ethan thought he saw some smoke come out of the duke's ears but figured that had to be his imagination. The duke, after all, wasn't a dragon, even if he acted like one.

"My finances are my business," Ethan said. "If I owed you money, it'd be one thing. But since I don't—"

"You are going to marry my daughter, and you have the nerve to be belligerent with me?" the duke yelled, rising to his feet.

Ethan jumped.

The duke hurried around the desk, and Ethan backed up to the door, relieved it was open. If the duke killed him, there would be witnesses. To his surprise, the duke came within a few inches of him and stopped. "My daughter is the most important thing in my life, and despite my wishes, I have to hand her over to you. As her father, I have a right to know that in addition to your corrupt lifestyle, you're not going to submit her to poverty!"

Ethan swallowed the lump in his throat and nodded. "All right." Her father made a good point. If Ethan had a daughter and thought she was about to end up with a pauper, he'd demand to see the steward, too.

The duke visibly relaxed.

Figuring that the sooner he relieved the duke's fears, the better, Ethan cleared his throat. "Then you'll be going with me to my townhouse?"

"I wouldn't dream of traveling anywhere with you. I'll go in my own carriage."

Why wasn't he surprised? Deciding not to comment, Ethan turned and followed her father out of the library. On their way to the front door, the footman opened it and Catherine and Lady Roderick stepped into the townhouse. They were laughing and holding a few expensive packages. No wonder the duke worried over his daughter's fate. She was a spendthrift! Well, that was no matter. He had more than enough money to keep her happily spending money for the rest of her life.

The ladies stopped when they saw the two gentlemen. "Father, what is he doing here?"

The disdain in Catherine's voice didn't go unnoticed. Ethan was ready to make an equally disdainful reply but decided against it since her father stood right next to him.

"I have some pressing matters to tend to," her father said. "I won't be gone long."

"You're leaving with him?" she asked, her eyebrows furrowed.

"Only for a short time. It's only business."

Resisting the urge to roll his eyes, Ethan greeted the ladies then went to his carriage. Once he was settled in his seat, he let out a weary sigh and closed his eyes. He honestly didn't know who upset him more. While this whole ordeal was his mother's fault, the duke and Catherine weren't helping matters at all. Granted, he could understand that they weren't happy. That was to be expected. But couldn't they at least make an effort to be nice?

In his mind, he got a glimpse of his upcoming marriage. His wife would see him as nothing but a rake and would shun him. His father-in-law would be looking over his shoulder, ready to examine every little thing he did or didn't do. And his mother would undoubtedly be hinting at an heir. He grimaced. His future was going to be a nightmare.

***

In the middle of May, Ethan and Catherine's close family and friends gathered at St. George's Church for the wedding, or rather, the disaster. Ethan tried not to notice the way the duke glared at him or the fact that Catherine sobbed relentlessly into a handkerchief. The whole thing was humiliating. The only person who was happy with the event was his mother who kept grinning from ear to ear.

Once the horrifying wedding was over, they went to the breakfast supper. He had to sit next to Catherine who continued to dab her eyes with a new handkerchief. At one point, he set down his fork and groaned.

"Will you please stop crying already?" he asked, wondering how many tears a lady could possibly have. Good heavens, but she must have cried a river at this point!

From her other side, her father directed his sharp gaze at Ethan. "What else would you expect from someone attending her own funeral?"

Just as Ethan was about to reply, his mother, who sat on his other side, patted his hand. Peering around him, she offered the duke a glowing smile. "It's normal for brides to cry."

"Those aren't tears of joy," Ethan muttered.

"Of course, they are. She just doesn't know it yet." She patted his hand again and looked at Catherine. "You'll love your bedchamber. I spared no expense in decorating it. Your furniture is made of rosewood. Oh, I can't express how beautiful it is to see chairs with such rich, deep brown color in them. They go so well with your peach bedding and curtains. Peach is such a soothing color, don't you think?"

Ethan gagged. Like he wanted to be subjected to talk of decorating bedchambers! "Mother, would you like to change seats so you can discuss this in detail?"

She laughed and waved her hand at him. "I wouldn't dream of separating you from your bride. This is your special day. It's a new beginning. Think of it as the first day of the rest of your life."

That made Catherine cry even harder.

"It's not working, Mother," Ethan replied, wondering why she insisted on acting so cheerful.

This was anything but a cheerful event, and all the food and music in the world wasn't going to lift the feeling of doom that hovered in the air. Even the guests, who consisted of a few family and friends were unusually quiet during the whole thing. And who could blame them? This really did seem like a funeral.

Ethan managed to finish his meal, not because it was easy to eat but because the food was good and no matter what the circumstance, he refused to let good food go to waste. He noticed that Catherine didn't bother to eat any of it, though she poked her food with her fork from time to time.

Meanwhile, Ethan's mother chatted with some of the guests about the fine decorations and the excellent music. They offered stilted replies while glancing warily at Catherine, but no one came right out and called the whole thing a farce so Ethan supposed it went as well as could be expected.

By the time it was over, Catherine's father asked to speak with Ethan. Though he didn't want to, he didn't dare upset him or Catherine any more than he already had, so he agreed.

Finding a secluded spot, her father clenched and unclenched his jaw. "This is a conversation I never wanted to have, but it appears I have no choice," he quietly said.

"Your Grace?" Ethan hesitantly asked, not sure where the other gentleman was going with this.

"It's not in my nature to be so bold, but my daughter is a delicate creature so I must."

Ethan couldn't argue that. He knew ladies were prone to crying and fainting, but Catherine was obnoxiously so. Every time she walked, she needed to lean against her father as if she didn't have the strength to manage on her own, and she was still crying. He'd be fortunate if she didn't fill his townhouse with her tears and float them all out to sea.

"Ethan," the duke began with a shudder, a silent indication that he hated thinking of Ethan as family but had to now that the wedding was over. After a long, and what Ethan suspected was an intentionally dramatic pause, the duke continued, "I must insist that you practice the utmost restraint tonight. You can't approach her as some common whore."

His jaw dropped. Was his father-in-law serious? Why was he having this discussion with him? And now? He glanced at the others who, thankfully, remained out of hearing distance.

"You will be gentle with her, and you'll be quick," the duke added. "Do I make myself clear?"

Unable to believe this was happening, he stared dumbly at him. He had no idea the duke could be so blunt. Good heavens. Between his mother and his father-in-law, he was being pestered from all angles!

"Well?"

The impatient tone in the duke's voice prompted him to respond. "Yes. Of course. I wouldn't dream of being any other way with your daughter."

The duke looked visibly relieved. "Good. I believe you'll do it."

Ethan remained still as the duke returned to his daughter. Never in his life did he think a wedding night could terrify a gentleman, but he was absolutely and completely terrified. He had no desire to be with Catherine in bed. All she'd do was cry. What gentleman wanted that? The whole thing made him sick to his stomach.

Well, there was an easy way to handle that. He wouldn't go to her bedchamber. Then he wouldn't have to force things along while she sobbed into her handkerchief. Relieved, he went to Catherine, forcing a smile to the guests who offered their congratulations.

When it was time to go to the carriage, Catherine wobbled on her feet and claimed she was weak, so his mother rushed to put her arm around her and steadied her. He knew it was awkward that his bride sought help from his mother, but it couldn't be helped. Even if his mother was the deceitful mastermind behind this travesty, Catherine would find more comfort with her than with him.

They entered the carriage and Catherine refused to sit next to him, so his mother sat between them. As the coachman led the horses forward, he shook his head and stared out of the small window. It was ridiculous. The guests had to be laughing over the whole ordeal. He knew he'd be laughing if he was watching it. He groaned and rubbed his eyes. Not only would he be laughing, but he'd hurry over to White's to tell the gentleman all about it.

"Ethan, it's bad manners to grumble when you're leaving your breakfast dinner," his mother admonished. "People are apt to think you don't want to be married."

"They'd be right," he hissed.

Catherine stopped sniffing into her handkerchief and glared at him. "I don't want to be married to you either!"

He made it a point to roll his eyes so she'd notice. Like everyone didn't already know that! "At least I didn't groan during the whole wedding and meal."

"I didn't groan."

"Your endless crying is just as bad."

His mother let out a hearty chuckle. "What you two need is time to sit and talk to each other. Once you do, you'll realize how ideal you are together."

He bit back his reply. It wouldn't do any good to argue. His mother refused to listen to reason. While his mother continued to console Catherine, he crossed his arms and turned his attention to the window. The irony wasn't lost to him. He'd spent the last five years carefully crafting his reputation in hopes of avoiding marriage, and yet it was his reputation that forced his mother to take such extreme measures. And now, he wasn't only married, but his marriage was already a dismal failure.

When the carriage finally came to a stop, he waited as the footman opened the door before daring a glance in his bride's direction. At least she wasn't crying anymore. Her eyes were swollen and her cheeks and nose red, but she wasn't crying so that was progress. After she and her mother stepped out of the carriage, he reluctantly followed them.

Though he'd love nothing more than to run off to White's, the taunting from the gentlemen there would be unbearable. "You swore you'd never marry," they'd say. "So much for your boasting!" Then they'd make bets on whether or not Catherine could tame him.

Well, he did have one small comfort. The townhouse was large enough where he could be alone, and he had his own bedchamber. When he entered the townhouse, the butler informed him that he had a package waiting for him in the library.

Surprised, he left his happy mother with her new daughter-in-law and went to the library to see what came for him.

He recognized the handwriting as soon as he saw the small box wrapped in brown paper. It was from Agatha. His curiosity piqued, he opened it. In the box was a jar of olive oil and a neatly folded paper. Even though he had a sinking sensation what the jar was for, he opened the letter and read it.

Before you disregard the jar, keep in mind I was married. Albeit, it was for almost twenty-four hours, but even so, I have experience in this area that you'll benefit from. Your wife's first time will most likely be disappointing. This isn't your fault. You don't know what to do. However, it works to your advantage that she doesn't know this. I'm afraid there's little you can do to relax a frightened young virgin, but you must not hop on top of her and stick it in right away. My advice is for you to touch and kiss all of her. Take time to adore her. Then put four to five drops of olive oil on your finger and slip it in the area between her legs. It'll make things more bearable for her, and she'll be more receptive to you next time you visit her bed.

Ethan quickly placed the jar back in the box and tore the letter so his mother and his new wife wouldn't read it. He closed the box and slipped it into the drawer of his desk. While other gentlemen might have been appalled at Agatha's boldness, he expected it from her. Sure, she wouldn't behave that way in polite society, but they both knew each other well enough to put aside such formalities when no one was around.

Even though he'd never admit it, he was relieved she gave him something to use to help the process go easier. He'd hate for Catherine to be so frightened over her first time that the duke would pick up on it. Granted, she would never tell him her first time was a disaster, but somehow—some way—Ethan knew her father would figure it out. The duke was a sly fox.

However, it wasn't an issue tonight, so Ethan could rest assured that, at the moment, he was safe from trying to make

Catherine's first time bearable enough where she wouldn't collapse into another bout of tears. He went over to the shelf, picked up his decanter and poured himself a glass of brandy. The day had been awful. He didn't know how it could get any worse, but he was sure if he spent any time with Catherine or his mother, it would. So he spent the rest of his time holed up in his library, reading a book.

Chapter Eight

Catherine accepted the tea from Ethan's mother and took a sip. The two were alone in the drawing room, and the closed door afforded them some privacy, giving her a much needed reprieve from her husband.

"You must not despair, Catherine," Ethan's mother softly said from where she sat next to her on the settee. "My son isn't as awful as he appears."

Though Catherine doubted it, she kept silent. Of course, a mother wouldn't think the worst about her son. To her, he was a darling cherub who did no wrong, no matter what scandalous deeds the *Tittletattle* reported about him.

"I know it's hard to believe," she continued as if she could read Catherine's thoughts, "but it's true. He's taken good care of me after his father passed on. I've never lacked for anything, and he's never spoken an ill word toward me. I expect he'll be the same way with you."

She sighed in despair. There was nothing she could do to get out of this marriage, and she couldn't believe any of the assurances his mother was giving her, though she wished she could. It'd make her feel better about this whole travesty.

"I want you to call me Rachel. We're family now, and I'd like for us to be friends. I hope it's all right that I call you Catherine?"

"You've been doing so already," she blurted out before she had time to think about it.

Rachel laughed. "I know, but it just occurred to me that I didn't ask. Given the circumstances of this wedding, I suddenly wondered if you'd want me to address you so informally."

"I suppose. It doesn't really matter." Not since she was now trapped in this family. She forced down a sip of tea.

"While we're alone and since you have no mother to address private matters with, I was wondering if you'd like me to explain what to expect in bed tonight."

Even as her curiosity nudged her to say yes, she wondered if it was wrong to agree. She lowered her gaze to her cup and ran her thumb along its handle. As a lady, she wasn't supposed to ask questions about such things. It was her duty to the crown. She understood that. She also understood it wasn't supposed to be something she'd enjoy. But even so, she was curious about the whole thing.

As if she hadn't noticed her hesitation, Rachel said, "I remember how nervous I was my first time. I gripped the bed sheets and kept darting glances at the door connecting my bedchamber with my husband's." She giggled. "When he came to my bedchamber, he took one look at me and left. I thought he was disappointed in me, but I later learned he was afraid he'd disappoint me."

"He was?"

Rachel laughed. "I didn't understand it either until he confided in me, but that wasn't until we'd been married for a year."

"It didn't take a year to...to..." Catherine couldn't bring herself to say the actual words, so she motioned for Rachel to continue.

"Oh, no. Thank goodness. Ethan was born fourteen months after we married. That wouldn't have happened if it'd taken his father a year to do his duty."

"How long did it take for him to do his…um…duty?"

"He made sure the marriage was consummated the next night because he knew he needed an heir. Our marriage had been arranged, so I barely knew him. He married me for my money. That was no secret. I think we hadn't spoken more than a few words to each other before the wedding. But I was very fortunate, for he turned out to be a wonderful gentleman." Rachel smiled at whatever memories played in her mind.

After a moment, Catherine ventured, "So how was it?" Her face warming from embarrassment over asking the question, she cleared her throat. "I mean, the wedding night."

"A bit of a disappointment, though I didn't realize that until later when I learned what I was capable of feeling when in bed with him. But I suspect it was because he was untried in the ways of a gentleman and lady when they're in bed."

"He was?"

"He was a couple years younger than me, so he hadn't had time to venture around town to seek his pleasure. His concern was marrying a lady to secure his financial affairs. His father left him in a terrible situation, so his guardian encouraged the match as soon as he turned eighteen."

Forgetting her nervousness, Catherine set her teacup on the table and turned to her. "And your father agreed?"

"I wasn't getting any younger, and I had no prospects. It was my only chance to marry, and I knew I better take it."

"Really?"

She chuckled. "I did my best to find a husband before then, I assure you. I suppose there was something about me that gentlemen didn't fancy."

"I find that hard to believe since you're so talkative. What I mean is that you're not shy. You can talk to anyone." It was something Catherine envied about her.

"That was part of my problem. I talked too much. I think most gentlemen prefer a lady who knows when to keep quiet.

Fortunately, Ethan's father enjoyed listening to me talk. He was a gentleman of few words. He said I could do the talking for both of us."

She smiled. "Then it seems like he was the perfect gentleman for you to marry."

"He was. I wouldn't have wanted to marry another. When I saw you at your father's ball, you reminded me of my dear husband. He had a tendency to find a quiet place to sit. He never enjoyed being the center of attention." She patted Catherine's hand. "Once you know what it's like to be in a good marriage, you don't want to settle for anything less. And I believe you and Ethan can have the same thing his father and I had. While I admit he has an undesirable reputation, he takes after me in other ways. I don't know if you've noticed the way he can talk to others, no matter how many people are gathered around him?"

"Yes, I did notice that." Catherine tapped her foot on the rug and took a deep breath before she blurted out, "Exactly what were the actions involved in your…time…with your husband?"

"Oh yes. I must get to that. You'll need to know it for tonight." She drank the rest of her tea and set the cup on the tray before focusing on her. "Gentlemen aren't built like us. Their chests are flat. Ours aren't."

"Mine is flatter than most women's."

"You needn't worry about that. As long as there's something, gentlemen are happy. There's another difference between them and us that makes them even happier. While we have nothing between our legs, they do."

Catherine knew she shouldn't be surprised by the lady's boldness, but her face went from warm to uncomfortably hot. And even as that was the case, she leaned toward Rachel in interest.

"I don't know how to describe it," Rachel continued. "At first glance, it's intimidating, but after you get used to it, you wonder why it seemed so imposing." With a shrug, she poured more tea in her cup. "Would you like some?"

Catherine shook her head, her heart hammering in her chest. "Imposing?"

"I apologize. I didn't mean to frighten you. I know you're nervous enough as it is." She set the teapot down and turned to face her. "It's an appendage. It's attached to them and its purpose is to go inside us so we can get a child. And don't be afraid if you notice it growing or shrinking. When the gentleman comes to bed, it's going to be longer than when he leaves. It has to be long enough to get inside. Do you understand?"

Uncertain, she gave a slight shake of her head.

Rachel sighed. "Maybe it's something you have to experience to understand. Well, perhaps the best thing to focus on is making the experience as painless as possible. There's not much you can do. Coming to the marriage as a virgin is a badge of virtue, of course, but I often thought it was highly unfair that ladies must endure some pain."

"Pain?" Why didn't her father warn her of this?

"Not to worry, dear. I snuck out some olive oil from the kitchen. While it's not the most pleasant thing to do, if you use some of this between your legs, it'll help the process along and hopefully lessen your discomfort. I put the oil next to your bed. I hid it under a hat I bought for you. There's no need to let the servants see it, but you're better off using it. Now, you mustn't be discouraged if your first time is disappointing. The best thing you can do is explore yourself to find out what you like or don't like, and then teach him what to do." She let out a low groan. "Though I suppose my son already knows how to please a lady."

Catherine stared at her, hardly believing her ears. Granted, Rachel wasn't known for acting inappropriately, but when no one was around, she was even bolder than Ethan. No wonder he turned out the way he did! Looking pleased, Rachel drank the rest of her tea. Unsure of what else to say, Catherine turned her attention back to her teacup and sipped her tea.

***

That night Catherine waited for Ethan to come to her bedchamber. She even left the candle on so he could find his way to her. She had the covers pulled up to her chin and wore her shift, but all she had to do was remove the covers and lift her shift and let him stick his thing into her.

After a long internal debate, she even used some of the olive oil his mother gave her. The process of putting it where it needed to be was messy and, for lack of a better term, disgusting, but she did it because she wished to make the consummation go faster and with as little pain as possible.

She was sure he would come to her bed before midnight. But when the clock chimed one, she let out a huff and threw the covers off of her so she could cross the room and go to the door connecting their bedchambers. He better not be out with someone else tonight! It was bad enough she had to marry him, but to be deserted on her wedding night in favor of another bed partner made her blood boil with rage. Of all nights, this was the one reserved for her. Her resolve strengthened, she flung the door open and entered his room.

To her surprise, he was asleep. He bolted up in his bed, his hair ruffled and his eyes wide. "I don't want to fence!" He blinked in the moonlight and rubbed his eyes. "Where am I?"

Seeing that as her cue, she rushed forward and stood by his bed. "Not with me, which is where you're supposed to be. Do I have to tell you what you're supposed to do on your wedding night?"

"I…uh…" He blinked several more times and stared at her. "I didn't think you'd want me to be with you tonight."

What did her wants have to do with anything? Her duty was to give him an heir. Exasperated, she sighed. "When were you planning on coming to my bed?"

He shrugged. "I don't know."

"You don't know!"

She placed her hands on her hips and glared at him, but the effect was probably lost on him since it was dark and he couldn't see much of her. Inspired, she went to his table and lit a candle. There. Now that he could properly see her disgust, she hurried back over to him and glared at him once more.

He rolled his eyes. "I was doing it for you. I thought you wouldn't want me in your bed, given how much you loathe me."

"This has nothing to do with how I feel about you."

"It doesn't?"

"No, it doesn't. We have a duty to the crown."

He groaned and placed his head in his hands. "You sound just like my mother."

Too annoyed to be nervous, she grunted and pulled her shift off. "I don't care if I sound like her or not. We're going to get this over with." She picked up his covers and nudged him in the side. "Move over so I can get in. I'll go back to my bed once you're done."

Chapter Nine

$\mathcal{F}$or the life of him, Ethan had no idea how Catherine ended up climbing into his bed. He went to sleep, like he did every night, and the next thing he knew, he was being woken up from a horrible nightmare where the Duke of Rumsey had invited him over for fencing—and he had a fiendish gleam in his eye as he made the invite. Even now, the dream chilled him to the bone. But Catherine was pushing at him to move over, taking his mind off of it.

Grunting as she accidently elbowed him in the side, he scrambled over to his side of the bed. "Ouch! You're hurting me."

"I'm sorry. I didn't mean to touch you."

He rolled his eyes. "You didn't mean to touch me? Good heavens, Catherine, isn't that why you're in here?"

She finally settled into a comfortable spot on the bed and cleared her throat. "I'm here to do my duty."

So she was determined to get this over with. Well, maybe it was better they did this now. Then she could go back to her own bed, and he could go back to sleep. He sighed and finally looked at her. She was lying next to him with the covers up to her neck. Resisting the urge to tell her that she'd need to lower the covers if she expected him to consummate the marriage, he slipped out of the bed to retrieve the jar of olive oil Agatha gave him.

"You're not leaving, are you?" she asked, sitting up.

Since she forgot to hold onto the covers, he got a good view of her perky breasts. Unable to take his eyes off the beautiful sight, he miscalculated where he was walking and stubbed his toe on the corner of the bed. He yelped in pain and grabbed his foot.

"You're not getting out of this," she said, crossing her arms, a process that only served to bring her breasts together. "Ethan!"

Surprised she said his name, he stopped rubbing his toe and directed his attention to her face. "What?"

"I said that I hope you don't think hurting your toe is a reason to delay what's supposed to happen tonight."

He rolled his eyes. "I don't think that."

If he did try getting out of consummating the marriage at this point, the duke would probably assume he preferred other ladies to his precious daughter. He thought Catherine would welcome his absence tonight, but now that he knew otherwise, it would behoove him to get the deed over with so she wouldn't run to her father about it. At least this way, she would learn the marital bed was dreadful for a lady and leave him alone. And who knew? Perhaps she'd conceive right away and that would be the end of it. Then his mother would be happy as well.

As he retrieved the jar from the cabinet, he couldn't help but think that everyone else was going to be happy about the consummation of his marriage except for him. He strode back to his side of the bed, determined to get this ordeal over with. Her father said he wanted him to be gentle and quick. He wondered just how quick "quick" was supposed to be.

He set the jar on the small table by his bed and, without looking at her, removed his clothes. When she gasped, he glanced at her. "What?"

"So that's what an appendage looks like."

He followed her gaze and saw his not-so-erect member. His face warm since it probably didn't seem that impressive in a flaccid state, he said, "It gets bigger. My toe still hurts, so I'm distracted." That and thinking of her father and his mother wasn't helping matters at all.

"It gets bigger? How do you make it bigger?"

Suddenly feeling awkward, he slipped under the covers so she was no longer staring at it. "I don't know. It just gets bigger."

"Can't you control it?"

"Not really."

"Why not? It's a part of your body."

She tried to lift the covers to see it again, but he placed his hands over the part of him she had referred to as his 'appendage'. "The proper term is penis."

"Penis?"

"There are other terms for it, but I never understood why they don't just call it what it is."

Leaning forward in interest, she asked, "What else can you call it?"

He paused, uncertain of how to answer her. "I don't think this is the kind of discussion we should be having," he finally replied.

"Why not? You're about to stick your appendage—penis—in me. I think I have a right to know what I can call it."

"You can call it what it is."

"I don't care for the word 'penis'. Certainly there must be a prettier word for it."

He looked at her in disbelief. A prettier word for penis? "A penis isn't supposed to have a pretty word for it. It's part of a gentleman's body, not a lady's."

"Let me see it again. Then I can think up a good term for it since you won't give me one."

She tried to get another look at it, but he held her hands to stop her from picking up the covers.

"Fine. Other terms are rod, pole...staff."

She scrunched her nose and shook her head. "I don't like any of those terms either."

"Then just call it what it is."

Catherine seemed disappointed but didn't press him further. Turning his attention to the table by the bed, he picked up the jar and removed the lid. "I got something to help you as we—" he struggled to find the right word—"consummate this marriage."

"What is it?"

"Just something to put down there, between your legs."

"Does that mean you'll be touching me?"

"I have to. This isn't something we can do apart from each other," he replied. "Do you understand what's going to happen?"

"Of course I do. I'm not as ignorant as you'd believe."

"You've done this before?"

Her eyes grew wide. "No. I wouldn't dare do such a thing and disgrace my father!"

"Then how do you know what's going to happen?"

"I've figured it out," she said, trying to appear nonchalant even as her face grew a pretty shade of pink.

"How is that possible when you didn't even know what a penis looked like?"

He waited for her to respond, but since she didn't, he guessed exactly how she knew. Leave it to his mother to stick her nose in where it didn't belong. Deciding to let the matter go, he pulled back the covers. Granted, it meant she could now see him, but there was little he could do about that. At least, he got a chance to see all of her, too, and he definitely liked what he was seeing.

"Your penis does get bigger," she commented, sitting up so she could more closely inspect him.

He'd been so busy checking out her breasts and the reddish-blonde triangle of curls between her legs that he hadn't noted his erection. Despite the fact that she was examining him with greater interest than he figured a virgin had the right to have, he poured five drops of olive oil on his fingers and grimaced. What was Agatha thinking in giving him this? Sure, it was slippery, but it made him think of food, not lovemaking.

He cleared his throat and motioned to the pillow. "You should lie down for this."

"Oh! Right."

She quickly obeyed, something he didn't expect her to actually do since she'd made it a habit of arguing with him. With a shake of his head, he ignored the way she inclined her head so she could still inspect him as he stretched out next to her. At least only one candle lit the room. Things were more romantic that way, as romantic as an awkward first time could be anyway. Truth be told, this had to be the most unromantic wedding night any couple could endure.

Pushing aside his apprehension, he brought his hand between her legs. "I think this would go easier if you spread your legs."

She looked up from his erection and nodded. "You're right. That thing can't go in me if I don't."

So they were now calling his penis a *thing*. Well, he could live with that. It was better than some 'pretty' name. He rubbed the oil between his fingers before brushing her entrance. She was soft and already slick, making it easy for him to insert a finger into her. He was surprised by how naturally he went into her. She shifted, an action which allowed him to slide deeper inside.

She let out a contented sigh and asked, "What are you putting in me?"

He considered lying to her because he didn't think she'd appreciate him using something only Cook was supposed to use, but he figured since it was her body, he better tell her the truth. She'd have to clean it all up later anyway. "It's olive oil. It's supposed to help you get ready for me."

"Olive oil? Why didn't you say so before? I already put some in there."

"What?"

"Your mother suggested it."

And that was when he lost his erection. "My mother?"

Unaware of the very unromantic effect the announcement had on him, she nodded. "I did as she suggested, so you don't need to do it again."

He shuddered and removed his finger from her so he could wipe the olive oil off on the covers. He immediately wished he had wiped it off on something else. Now he'd need to have his covers washed so it wouldn't smell like the kitchen when he slept.

"What's wrong?" she asked.

"What's wrong? You're serious about asking me what's wrong?"

"I wouldn't have asked the question if I wasn't."

"It's not...good...when you mention my mother while we're in bed."

"But I'm trying to help you. There's no need to put more olive oil in me."

"I can't do this tonight," he finally said. As embarrassing as it was to admit, he knew he was better off just coming out and saying it. Why go through any more torture than they'd already endured?

She gasped and sat up. "But we have to! It's our wedding night."

"We can do it tomorrow night. Just don't put olive oil in you. I'll do it next time."

"Ethan!" She reached for him as he turned to get off the bed and pulled him into her arms. "I can't be a virgin after tonight. It'll be a disgrace. My duty is to get this done."

"I don't know if I can get it done," he argued as he fell back next to her. She was lying partially over him now, successfully pinning him down. "There's too much pressure."

"But you've done this many times. If you can do this with other ladies, why can't you do it with me?"

"I haven't done it before. With anyone." As soon as he said the words, he wished he could take them back. The shame! The horror! Why couldn't he keep his big mouth shut? Looking at her stunned expression, he weakly asked, "You won't tell anyone, will you?"

"Are you telling me you can't consummate the marriage at all? Your penis won't stay big long enough to go into me?"

His jaw dropped. Good heavens, that was worse than being a virgin! "I'm not impotent! It's just that when we're talking about my mother, it's impossible to do it."

"We won't talk about her anymore. It's just you and me. What can I do to make you get bigger so we can do this tonight?"

He groaned and stared at the ceiling. "It's not something I can force. It happens on its own."

"But there must be something I can do to help." She scanned his body, her gaze settling on his limp member. Looking at him again, she said, "I promise I won't tell anyone that you haven't been intimate with a lady before. I'll keep your secret."

"Well…" He ventured a glance in her direction and realized she meant it. She wouldn't reveal the truth. "I spent a lot of time convincing everyone I was a rake."

"I know you did. You had me convinced."

"I don't want anyone to know the truth."

"No one will. I just told you I would keep your secret. Do you doubt I'll keep my word?"

He studied her serious expression and relaxed. "No, no I don't doubt you."

She smiled. It suddenly occurred to him that in all the time he'd known her, he'd never seen her genuinely smile. She'd offered the obligatory smiles when they'd been at balls. She'd also given the same type of smile to other gentlemen, so he knew it was something she did to everyone. But now as she smiled at him, he realized there was more to her than anyone else knew about.

He brought his hand up to cup the side of her face and brushed her cheek with his thumb. Her skin was soft. In fact, as he took careful note of her face, he realized she had a smooth complexion. Her cheeks were slightly flushed, her deep brown eyes twinkled in the candlelight, and her hair cascaded over her shoulders in gentle curls. Why hadn't he noticed how appealing she was before?

He brought her face toward his and caressed her lips with his. Warmth spread through his body, and he felt a stirring in his loins. Encouraged, he deepened the kiss. This was much better than their trite kiss at the wedding. Of course, that kiss was in front of everyone, and she'd been crying at the time. But she wasn't crying now. In fact, she was responding quite nicely to his advances.

She shifted into a more comfortable position, an action which allowed her breasts to press against his chest, something which caused him to finally become fully erect. Now this was more like it. He wrapped her in his arms and brought her fully on top of him. His erection settled between her legs, and she let out a slight gasp of surprise but he kept his lips on hers so she wouldn't get shy and pull away from him. Not that he knew whether she'd pull away from him or not, but why take the chance?

He brushed her lower lip with his tongue and was delighted when she parted her lips for him. Accepting her invitation, he interlaced his tongue with hers. She tasted wonderful. He lowered his hands and traced the sides of her breasts then went lower to her hips. He moved her hips and was rewarded as she rubbed up against his arousal. She felt wonderful. So very wonderful.

Still kissing her, he embraced her and rolled over, taking her with him so that she was under him. She wrapped her legs around his waist, her flesh beckoning him to enter her. He wasn't sure what to do. Well, that wasn't entirely true. He knew he was supposed to enter her in order to consummate the marriage, but another part of him wanted to explore more of her first.

Then he unwittingly recalled her father's warning to make it quick. He pulled away from her for a moment and scanned the bedchamber, just to make sure that her father wasn't hovering in the shadows somewhere.

"Is something wrong?" she asked, her breathing heavy.

Shaking off the strange sensation that her father was somehow watching them, he turned his attention back to her and took the moment to look at her body. What in the world made him think she was ordinary? She was the most exquisite creature he'd ever seen. He cupped one of her breasts in his hands and brushed her hardened nipple with his thumb. She shivered under him, and he glanced at her, relieved when he saw that she had her eyes closed and that her mouth was turned up into a slight smile. Good. She didn't shiver because she was repulsed that he'd touched her so intimately.

Further encouraged, he lowered his head to her breast and traced her nipple with his tongue. This resulted in the lovely sound of her moaning as she tightened her hold on his arms. This was even better. Who knew Catherine could be so passionate? Sure, he knew she could passionately detest the idea of being married to him, but it was much better when she was passionate about being in his bed. He didn't dare question it. At the moment, he was more aroused than he thought possible, and he didn't want to break the spell that had fallen between them.

He settled back on top of her so that his erection was between her legs, pressed ever so nicely against her. He shifted and his tip centered on her entrance. She moved her hips in silent encouragement and kissed his shoulder, her fingers digging into his arms in a way that excited him. She wanted him. Really wanted him. He groaned in pleasure and brought his mouth to hers, and this time his tongue was more insistent as he explored her.

She lifted her hips and her legs pulled him closer to her, and given how moist she was, he slid into her until he came to a part of her that was tight. He wanted to pause, to figure out what he should do, but her flesh was much too enticing and he had no control. He pushed into her, and they both gasped. But it didn't sound like her gasp was the same as his. It seemed as if she gasped in pain.

His eyes flew open and he looked at her. There was a slight grimace on her face, and in that split second, he saw the condemning look on her father's face for hurting her. Before he lost the little control he'd managed to gather, he pulled out of her and noticed that she was bleeding. He couldn't be sure how much blood there was, but it was enough to convince him this wasn't good. He could only hope she wouldn't tell her father he hurt her.

He rested on his back and wondered if he should even attempt to look at her. Would she be crying? Would she be fuming with rage?

"Is that it?" she asked.

Surprised by the bewildered tone in her voice, he dared a peek in her direction. Thankfully, she didn't have tears in her eyes, and she wasn't frowning at him. Instead, her eyes were wide, and she rolled on to her side to look at him.

He wasn't sure how to answer her. While he hadn't finished, imagining how upset her father would be to know he'd hurt her was enough to make him not-so-erect again. He really hated this. He had no idea being in bed with a lady demanded so much of him. If he didn't remain erect, the whole thing was impossible.

"Ethan, is that it?"

He should've known she wouldn't let the matter go just because he didn't want to answer her. With a reluctant sigh, he asked, "Do you want me to keep going when I just made it painful for you?"

She rose up on her elbow and peered down at him. "I thought it was supposed to hurt the first time."

"That makes no sense."

"It's something ladies go through, but it wasn't that bad."

"Wasn't that bad? You're bleeding." He motioned to the area between her legs. "Down there."

She checked between her legs. "It's only a little bit."

"It shouldn't be there at all."

"I've suffered far worse than this." When he shook his head, she continued, "I have. Once a month, I endure far greater pain than what I did just now, and that lasts for hours if I don't drink the right tea as soon as my cycle starts."

He pressed his hands to his ears and cringed. "All right. You've convinced me." Good heavens! Was there nothing she wouldn't tell him?

She removed one of his hands from his ear. "Does such talk disturb you?"

"Of course it does."

"I'm sorry. I won't say any more about my monthly flow."

"Thank you." He lowered his other hand and set it on his stomach.

"Do you want to finish?"

"Not right now," he said. "I'd rather wait until you don't feel any pain at all before we try this again."

She frowned in disappointment. "But I wanted to get this done tonight."

"We did. Well, we did enough. You're not a virgin anymore."

"So we finished?"

How could he explain it to her without embarrassing her? He glanced at her. Forget embarrassing her. He didn't want to embarrass himself! All these years, he never once took himself for a prude, and yet, he was finding out just how prudish he was.

He offered a helpless shrug and said, "No, we didn't finish, but since I penetrated you, you're not a virgin. That's why you bled. But I'm not ready to do this again right now."

"So when will you be ready?"

"I don't know."

"You don't have any idea at all?"

"No, I don't, but when I am, my body will let me know." She opened her mouth to speak, but he kissed her. "Blow out the candle, so we can go to sleep. All right?"

Despite her disappointment, she nodded and did as he asked. He took her into his arms and closed his eyes. It was nice to hold her. Even if he couldn't get the image of her scowling father out of his mind, it was still nice to have her in his arms. Exhausted from the day's events, he soon drifted off to sleep, only to wake up periodically through the night with dreams of her father challenging him to a duel.

Chapter Ten

Catherine woke up alone, and for a moment, she thought it'd been a strange dream. But the slight ache between her legs and the fact that she was in Ethan's bed proved that the previous night's events really did happen. She sat up in bed and glanced around the room. Where was her husband? She'd hoped he would finish consummating their marriage this morning, but that wasn't going to happen as long as he wasn't with her.

Deciding not to spend the day waiting to see if he'd return since he most likely wouldn't, she got out of bed, retrieved her shift and hurried to her bedchamber. She requested that a bath be brought up as soon as her lady's maid entered the room, and when the maids filled the tub with soothing warm water, she stepped into it.

She leaned back in the tub and closed her eyes. She hadn't slept much the night before. Her efforts to fully consummate the marriage had been in vain. She didn't understand why it should be so difficult for Ethan to go through with it. Sure, it had hurt when he put his penis into her, but it hadn't been as devastating as he made it out to be. She rolled her eyes. It was a good thing he wasn't a lady. If he was squeamish about a little blood, he'd never survive the monthly flow.

But it was sweet that he didn't want to hurt her, so she shouldn't be critical of him. She had her heart set on completing the act, and it didn't happen. Sure, she was disappointed, but it wasn't the worst thing that ever happened to her. It would help if she knew when they'd do the entire deed from start to finish, but if he had no control over his penis, then what could she do? She had no way of making it big, so she couldn't help him along. The thing seemed to have a mind of its own, and there seemed to be no predicting when it was ready to enter her. She wondered what happened when the act was done.

Opening her eyes, she turned her attention to the soap and picked it up from the nearby table. One thing she definitely had to do was wash up between her legs. As she cleaned up, she recalled the way Ethan made her feel while he was touching her. She'd enjoyed the way his hands and tongue felt on her breasts, of course. She definitely wanted him to do that again, but when he caressed the area between her legs, the pleasure was more intense. She hadn't even known her body was capable of producing such sensations until he touched her.

Curious, she took the time to explore herself, wondering what it was Ethan had felt. If she hadn't been so nervous when she was putting the olive oil in herself, she might have noticed how sensitive she was. But now she did notice, and she noticed other things as well. How her body's heat rose, how her breathing grew shallower, how the pleasure increased until it peaked in a way she never anticipated, and how her body hummed in satisfaction when it was over. Truly, she had no idea what Ethan was starting last night could lead to such bliss!

Once she gathered her composure, she thought of being with Ethan again. She finished washing herself off, thinking of what she might say or do to encourage him to come to her bed that night. It was too early in the day to lead him to her bedchamber now, but even so, she needed to have a plan. Somehow, someway, she was going to get him to finish what he started if it was the last thing she did.

***

"Why aren't you doting over your bride?"

Ethan slammed *The Canterbury Tales* shut and shoved the book behind the pillow on his chair. Standing up, he turned to face his mother. "Can't you knock before you barge into my sanctuary?"

His mother stepped into the library and shook her head. "This isn't your sanctuary. It's where you come to read books you know I wouldn't approve of."

"Seriously, Mother. Why do you assume I'm reading something inappropriate?"

"I won't justify that question with an answer," she replied, crossing her arms and scanning the room. "Sometimes I miss your father. There were times I'd come into this room and…" She glanced at him and shrugged. "Well, he didn't consider this room off limits to me."

Ethan grimaced. "If I am a rake, it's because I have you for a mother. You have no more sense of propriety than I do. The only difference is, you hide it from the Ton."

"What your father and I did wasn't wrong."

"I don't want to know what you two did." Eager to change the topic, he asked, "Did you come to discuss my reading habits again?"

She made a sign of the cross and shook her head. "No. I only hope your wife won't stumble upon such…such… You know."

He resisted the urge to laugh. After last night, he doubted that Catherine would be so appalled by books his mother deemed inappropriate…if he had them. She'd probably insist on reading them to satisfy her curiosity.

The butler entered the library. "The Duke of Rumsey is here, my lord."

Ethan blanched.

"What's he doing here so early?" Ethan's mother asked, not hiding her surprise.

Ethan groaned. "Isn't it obvious?" Ignoring her response, he sighed and told the butler. "He's here to make sure his daughter isn't still crying." He could only hope Catherine wouldn't say anything to her father about being disappointed with him. With a resigned sigh, he said, "Make sure there's a place for him at the breakfast table."

Once the butler left, his mother turned to him and smiled. "How wonderful!"

"It's not wonderful," he muttered. "He's not here on friendly terms."

She waved her hand at him and shook her head. "You need to have more faith, Ethan. Today might be awkward, but I assure you that soon enough, you'll be on good terms with him."

Unable to believe her unwarranted optimism, he passed her so he could leave the room. Maybe he could sneak upstairs and plead with Catherine to pretend like she was content so her father wouldn't panic. As he turned for the staircase, he heard Catherine welcoming her father at the entryway. Blast it! Forcing back a frustrated scream, he straightened and approached the two.

"Are you sure you're all right?" her father asked her.

Catherine nodded. "Father, I already told you I'm fine."

He examined her face with a worried frown. "You're not just saying that to ease my nerves, are you?"

"No, I'm not. I really am fine."

He breathed an audible sigh of relief. "I couldn't sleep at all last night. I kept seeing you being pursued by that husband of yours."

Ethan halted his steps and stared at the duke in disbelief. Pursued? If anyone was pursuing anyone last night, she was pursuing him!

Catherine giggled and hugged her father. "You have nothing to worry about."

"That's very brave of you to say," he said when the hug ended. "You have your mother's courage. She was able to put on a smile no matter how dour the situation."

Ethan's mother passed by him in the hall and hurried over to Catherine and her father. "Why, Your Grace, how thoughtful of you to come over, even if the hour is early for visits."

"I couldn't rest," he replied, standing close to his daughter. "I had to make sure my daughter is all right." He turned his concerned gaze in her direction as if he didn't believe her smile was genuine.

"We're glad to have you here, aren't we, Ethan?" his mother asked, turning to face him.

Catherine and her father finally looked at him. Since he wasn't particularly happy that her father was there, he settled for a slight shrug.

"He's delighted," his mother told the duke who frowned at him. "We're just about to have breakfast. The buffet is ready. All you have to do is pick what you want."

Though Ethan prayed the duke would say no and leave, the duke offered a nod, indicating his agreement to stay, at least for breakfast. As his mother cheered, Ethan's gaze went skyward, and he wondered why God seemed to be so reluctant to answer any of his prayers.

"Will you escort me to breakfast?" Catherine asked.

At first, Ethan thought she was talking to her father, but when everyone directed their attention to him, he realized she had asked him the question. "Pardon?" he dumbly replied, wondering why she didn't want her father to escort her instead.

Catherine walked over to him and stood beside him. "I'm ready when you are."

His mother clapped her hands in excitement while the duke's scowl deepened.

"Perhaps you'd like to escort Ethan's mother?" Catherine suggested with an expectant look on her face as she stared at her father.

The duke forced a smile and extended his arm toward Ethan's mother. "If I may have the honor?"

"I'd be delighted, Your Grace," Ethan's mother replied and accepted his arm.

Ethan waited until the two passed him before he led Catherine to breakfast. This was going to be one very awkward, and long, meal.

And as it turned out, he was right. During the meal, the only person who spoke was his mother. Everyone else remained quiet. Across from him, the duke never once took his eyes off of him. His mother either didn't notice or pretended not to notice.

Next to him, Catherine sat a little too close to him, but he didn't dare move away from her in case her father assumed he was repulsed by her. However, nothing could be farther from the truth. He was seeing her in a new light this morning. After everything that transpired last night, she'd told her father she was doing well, and he appreciated it, especially since she hadn't known he was within hearing distance.

"Wouldn't it be lovely if Ethan took Catherine on a carriage ride?" his mother droned on. "Maybe they could take a walk through Hyde Park. It's so lovely this time of year! I remember when Ethan's father took me there shortly after we married. He was terribly shy and..."

Ethan's mind wandered off. He'd heard this story enough already. It was the day he bought her some flowers and when the wind blew them out of her hands, he chased after them. Unfortunately, he wasn't an astute observer to what was going on around him and ended up running into a horse and getting injured for a couple of weeks. She was so touched because he went to all that trouble to retrieve her flowers that she fell in love with him. Ethan supposed, to a lady, it was a romantic tale, but he often thought his father was foolish to go chasing some flowers when he could have just bought another bouquet. It wasn't like he didn't have the money to do so.

A hand touched his leg, and Ethan almost dropped his fork. He looked at Catherine who continued eating her eggs as if she hadn't reached under the table to rest her hand on his thigh.

"When you've been loved the way I have, you appreciate how special marriage can be," Ethan's mother continued. "Your Grace, did you love your wife?"

For the first time since they started eating, the duke took his eyes off of Ethan. "Yes, I did."

"Then aren't we fortunate? So few find a love match," his mother replied, seeming pleased that the duke had something in common with her.

He turned his attention to his plate and ate a strawberry.

Undisturbed by his lack of response, she rambled on about the virtues of love. Ethan noticed the duke's grimace, but then Catherine distracted him by squeezing his thigh. He resisted the urge to look at her again in case he caught her father's attention.

"One thing I've learned," his mother went on, "is that you must make the most of every day we're given because you don't know when the day is going to be your last. There's no use in dwelling on how things might have been. Enjoy what you have while you have it." She grinned at Ethan and Catherine. "You two will do well together. I just know it."

He ventured a glance at Catherine then and was surprised when she offered his mother a smile in return. She had a lovely smile. He'd much rather see her smile than cry. When she smiled because she was happy, her face lit up in a way that made her look radiant. One could only guess why she was happy this morning. It wasn't anything he did. Perhaps it was his mother. Granted, his mother had a tendency to mind others' businesses and manipulate things to her advantage, but she had a good heart and only wanted the best for those she loved. Maybe his mother had found a way to befriend her.

Across the table, Catherine's father wiped his mouth and placed the napkin neatly on the table next to his plate. He leaned forward and made eye contact with Ethan. "Before you and my daughter spend any more time together, I want to speak to her in private."

Catherine rubbed Ethan's thigh. "I told you I'm fine. Besides, shouldn't I spend the day with my husband as my mother-in-law suggested?"

"I've been your father longer than *he's* been your husband," he told her.

Ethan forced down the last of his tea, trying not to notice that her hand was steadily moving up his thigh. For the life of him, he didn't understand her at all. Weren't virgins supposed to be timid? Everything he'd ever heard assured him of this fact, and yet she insisted on being overly familiar with him—and in a public setting of all places.

And worse, his body responded to her. He recalled how wonderful she'd felt when he entered her, and even as her father's eyebrows furrowed in disapproval, he had this ridiculous urge to pick her up and haul her off to his bedchamber. Maybe this time, it wouldn't be painful for her.

"Father," Catherine began, "I don't know what else we can say to each other that hasn't already been said. Why don't I pay you a visit later this week?"

When the duke opened his mouth to speak, Ethan's mother chimed in. "I'm sure it'd put your father's mind at ease if you'd talk to him," she gently told Catherine.

Catherine turned her gaze to Ethan, and he wondered if she had any idea that he was fully erect? Probably not, though he had no doubt she was aiming for that very thing. "Maybe you should go to your gentleman's club."

"I don't think that's a good idea," her father protested.

"There's no reason for him to stay here, unless you want him to stay in his library and be bored," she replied.

The duke grunted under his breath. "There are worst things he could do with his time than spend it reading a book."

Ethan's mother looked heavenward but didn't say anything, thankfully. He knew what she was thinking. She assumed he would spend his morning reading something inappropriate.

Catherine groaned. "Truly, Father, everything will be all right." She directed her gaze to Ethan. "I trust you."

Ethan's heart warmed at her admission.

But before he could respond, her father crossed his arms and shook his head. "I have sheltered you a little too well. All right. If this is what you wish, then let him go to the gentleman's club." His eyes met Ethan's and he added, "I trust you'll find a game of chess or political talk to your liking."

Hardly. But Ethan wouldn't admit that. Because he was expected to, he indicated his agreement with a slight nod.

"Then it's settled." Catherine removed her hand from his thigh—an action which disappointed him, though at least now he would be able to stand up without an erection—and quickly finished the last of her fruit. "We'll go anywhere you want to go later on today," she told Ethan.

"Anywhere respectable," the duke muttered, glaring at Ethan.

Ethan fought the urge to reply. Even if he wasn't the rake everyone believed him to be, he wouldn't dare take Catherine somewhere that wasn't appropriate for a lady. True, she wasn't acting much like he expected a lady to act, but she still had delicate sensibilities...or at least, he assumed she did.

As they rose from the table, she told her father, "I have something I must tell Ethan before he leaves. I won't be long."

"Can't it wait?" Ethan asked when he noticed the displeasure on the duke's face.

"No, it's rather urgent."

She took his hand and led him out of the room before anyone could protest. She practically dragged him down the hall and for a minute, he thought she was going to lug him up to the bedchamber, and he'd be lying if he said the prospect didn't thrill him. But she took him to the library and shut the door. He wanted to ask her what was so important that she had to talk to him right now, but she brought her arms around his neck and kissed him.

The action startled him, so he didn't respond right away. Undaunted by his reaction, she continued kissing him. Her body pressed against his, and he fell back against the door. She felt as wonderful today as she had last night. He embraced her and deepened the kiss, recalling how beautiful she was when she was naked. Sure, she was pleasing to the eye when she wore clothes, but she was much more so without them on.

She parted her lips, and his tongue brushed hers. Letting out a soft moan, she rubbed herself seductively against him. By now, his erection was demanding to be freed from the confines of his clothing. Still kissing him, she pulled away from him enough so that she could run one of her hands along the length of his arousal. He groaned his appreciation and cupped her breasts in his hands.

"Are you in any kind of pain?" he whispered in her ear, delighting in the way she stroked him.

"No," she softly replied, her breathing as shallow as his. "I feel good down there, Ethan. I want you inside me."

To emphasize her point, she unbuttoned his breeches and slid her hand into the opening to better fondle him. By now it was evident she wasn't the timid young bride he expected her to be, and quite frankly, he was exceedingly glad for his good fortune. What gentleman, after all, wanted a frigid wife?

He wanted nothing more than to strip her of her clothes and plunge deep inside her, and this time, he wouldn't stop until he released his seed into her. He entertained the idea in his mind but knew he couldn't actually do it now, not with her father somewhere in the house waiting for her.

He groaned, and this time it was in agony as she kissed his neck. "We can't. Not now. Not with your father here."

"I know." She brought her mouth to his ear and traced it with her tongue, sending a thrill of pleasure straight to his groin. "I just wanted a prelude to tonight," she whispered. Then she pulled away from him and buttoned his breeches back up. "I also wanted to feel your penis."

That part of his body was straining hard to get back into her hands, not at all happy that it was, once again, confined inside his clothes. He swallowed hard and watched as she adjusted her morning dress. Her cheeks were flushed, her eyes twinkling with excitement, and her heavy breathing made her breasts more prominent than they'd ever been.

"My goodness, you're beautiful," he murmured, taking in the full sight of her.

She shot him a delighted smile. "You really think so?"

She could stand there, knowing full well how hard he was, and ask him that? "Of course."

"Ethan, I am so sorry for all those years I misjudged you." She leaned forward and gave him a chaste kiss. "I can't keep my father waiting. Knowing how determined he is to talk to me, he'll probably break down the door if I don't scurry out of here. But I want to assure you that I meant what I said last night. I won't tell anyone that you've never been in bed with a lady until last night. I'll also assure him that I haven't been traumatized after our wedding night."

"Traumatized?" Her father told her he thought being with her husband would traumatize her? Even if the duke thought he was a rake, this was ridiculous!

"As you can see, I'm doing fine. And tonight when we finish what we started, I'll be even better." She winked at him and gently pushed him aside so she could open the door. Lowering her voice, she added, "I am aching down there, but it's because I need you in me, not because I'm in any kind of pain."

She slipped out of the room and shut the door softly behind her. He stood there for a long moment, his heartbeat still fast, his body still hard with need, and his breathing still ragged. How was it possible she had this affect on him? He knew being with a lady this way would arouse him, but he had no idea he could get this excited. He leaned against the door and looked at his erection.

"You'll have to wait until tonight," he told it.

It ached in protest.

"Don't blame me. You're the one who couldn't stay hard last night."

What was he doing? Talking to his penis? That was it. He was going to be locked away in an asylum if he didn't get a handle on being married to Catherine. She had him acting irrationally. Gentlemen didn't go around talking to parts of their bodies. He closed his eyes and took a couple deep breaths to calm himself—and the impatient part of his body—down. After a few minutes, he finally relaxed, and he could safely venture outside the room without bringing attention to how eager he was to be in bed with his wife. Deciding a trip to White's wasn't such a bad idea since it would help take his mind off of her, he hurried out of the townhouse.

Chapter Eleven

Catherine poured tea into her father's cup as Ethan left the townhouse. The area between her legs ached to continue what she'd started in the library and her nipples hardened at the reminder of how his hands felt on her breasts. She hoped her plan to finish consummating the marriage tonight was successful. She wanted to explore the pleasures waiting for her in bed with Ethan.

"Catherine?" her father asked, breaking her out of her thoughts.

Blushing, she forced her attention back to him. "What is it, Father?"

Though he accepted the cup she offered him, he didn't drink anything. He leaned back in his chair and studied her. "I blame myself for this."

"For what?" She poured tea into her own cup.

"The marriage. I should have protested more that night of the ball."

She sipped her tea, ever thankful he hadn't fought harder. Sure, she was devastated at the time. Yesterday morning, she believed her life was over. But after learning that Ethan hadn't known a lady intimately, she was thrilled. She liked knowing he'd only touched and kissed her in places that made her body feel more wonderful than she thought possible. She now understood he hadn't come to her bed because he was shy. It wasn't because he'd rather been with a lady who knew how to pleasure him. Since they were both new to the bedroom, they could learn what they liked together. It gave them something in common.

And besides, he'd called her beautiful. He'd touched and kissed her, leaving her breathless. There was no mistaking the desire in his eyes when he'd looked at her in the library. He wanted her. Wanted her in a way she never imagined any gentleman would. Better yet, he worried that he might hurt her, and she liked that most of all. Even if they hardly knew each other, she understood he had a tender heart.

"Catherine?"

Blinking, she turned back to her father. "What?"

"I hope you don't hate me."

She laughed and placed her cup on the tray. "I don't hate you. You're my father."

"But am I good one?"

"Of course, you are. You always have been."

"I don't feel like I am. I could barely eat anything yesterday. I kept seeing you crying as you went off with...with...him."

"He has a name."

He let out a weary sigh. "You don't have to pretend, Catherine. I know you're trying to make me feel better about forcing you into this marriage. You were very much the lady at breakfast, being polite with him and his mother."

"Ethan and his mother have been kind to me."

"You don't have to lie to make me feel better."

Surprised, she chuckled. "I'm not lying. It's the truth."

By the way he rubbed his forehead, she realized he wouldn't believe her, no matter what she said. Well, she tried. If he refused to believe her, there wasn't anything she could do about it. She sipped her tea and smiled at him. Bless his heart all the same. He loved her and wanted to do everything he could to protect her.

"I don't hate you," she assured him. "You're a good father."

"That's very sweet of you to say, but I wasn't diligent at the ball. If I was, he wouldn't have been able to get near you."

She took another sip of her tea. "Is there anything I can do to help you feel better?"

He wryly grinned at her. "I should be asking you that question."

In the past, whenever he worried that he had disappointed her, he liked to buy her gifts to ease his conscience. Thinking that might work in this situation, she set the cup down and rose to her feet. "I wouldn't mind a stroll through the Pantheon Bazaar."

To her relief, his eyes lit up as he quickly placed his full cup on the tray then stood up. "I'll get you anything your heart desires."

"If you insist," she replied, knowing full well he would.

"Of course, I insist. You need to let me make this disastrous marriage up to you." He went over to her and kissed the top of her head. "Your mother always felt better when she went shopping. This will be just the thing to ease your pain."

"All right."

Relaxing, he smiled and hugged her. "You can get anything you want."

She knew that, too, and she would make sure whatever she picked out would be expensive enough to assure him that he was still a good father.

***

Ethan gulped his glass of port wine and set it on the table next to the chessboard. What made him think that coming to White's was a good idea? Oh right. Catherine wanted him to come here and enjoy his morning away from her father and his mother.

"I've never seen you drink wine that fast," Christopher said in amusement as he leaned back in the seat across from him. "Your wife is causing you trouble already?"

"You have no idea," he muttered.

Ethan couldn't concentrate on anything. He'd tried reading the newspaper, which bored him anyway but even more so today. Then he attempted a game of chess with Christopher, but he couldn't focus on which pawn was doing what. His mind kept going back to the library where she was kissing him, rubbing her delectable body up against him, and fondling his erection. Then she left the room, leaving him unsatisfied. And to make matters worse, the alcohol was settling in his loins, furthering his desire to be with her. It was too much for a gentleman to take. No gentleman should have to suffer so!

Christopher shook his head and chuckled. "Tell me, what is it like being married to the Duke of Rumsey's daughter? No one can tell what she's really like under her hard shell. Is she as aloof as she seems?"

Ethan snorted. "No. That aloofness is a mask. The lady has no qualms about letting a gentleman know exactly what she wants when there's no one else around."

"But she seems so docile every time I've seen her."

"That's probably what she wants people to think." He took his pocket watch out and glanced at it. He'd only been here for twenty minutes? He used to come here for hours and not notice the passage of time. And yet today, time was passing at an irritatingly slow pace. Slipping the watch back into his pocket, he crossed his legs. "I never should have gotten married."

Christopher laughed. "Don't you think you're exaggerating your misery a little too much? Just because you're married, it doesn't mean you can't continue to enjoy life. Tell some raunchy jokes, play a few card games in the other room, or run off to dally with a lady or two."

"I don't feel like it."

"I don't understand how one day of marriage has killed your spirit. Other gentlemen get married and act as if nothing is different."

Ethan crossed his arms and sighed. "It's not that I dread being with her. On the contrary, I rather enjoy it."

His eyes grew wide and he leaned forward. "You do?"

"Lower your voice!" he hissed. "I'm only telling you because you're a trusted friend." Though he'd never reveal that his reputation with the ladies was only a pretense, he didn't mind telling him how much his wife confounded him. "As it turns out, she's quite…pleasant."

"Surely, you jest."

Ethan shook his head.

"But she spent all her time crying at the wedding breakfast. I saw it for myself. A couple couldn't be more mismatched."

"We were mismatched." Maybe they still were, except in a way he hadn't anticipated. "She spent the entire day sulking because she had to marry me."

"Yes, that's what I remember. And you looked like a fox trapped in a hole."

"Please assure me that I didn't look like that."

"I'm afraid you did."

Ethan grimaced. That wasn't the way he wanted to appear to others. While he felt that way, he honestly believed he was able to mask his feelings better than that.

"No one could blame you. You were marrying the Duke of Rumsey's daughter," Christopher replied.

"You say that as if it's a bad thing."

He shrugged as he collected the chess pieces. "Isn't it?"

"No, not really."

"If she isn't as dreadful as you feared, then why are you upset? You should be spending the day with her instead of being here. I know I'd rather be with a lady than a bunch of stuffy gentlemen."

"You don't like White's?"

"It's all right. It's somewhere to go that won't cause me trouble with my guardian, but I'd rather be in the company of a good lady."

"What an odd pair we are," Ethan mused. "You're eager to get married, and I didn't want to be married at all."

"My guardian's friend, Lord Roderick, is married, and he's one of the happiest gentlemen I've seen."

"Lord Roderick's situation could only improve with marriage given how dull he is. All he does is talk about politics. There's more to life than what's going on in Parliament."

Christopher nodded as he put the chess pieces where they belonged so someone else could start a game after they left. "I don't particularly care for him myself."

"I suppose not after he made you clean chamber pots."

"His wife is his only redeeming quality."

"At least he's not your guardian."

"Thank goodness for small favors, though he can be meddlesome."

"If your guardian found a wife," Ethan began, "he wouldn't have time to meddle in your life. Maybe you should find him a lady."

"I don't know. He doesn't seem interested in getting married." After a slight pause, he asked, "Are you going to Lord and Lady Martin's ball?"

"I hadn't planned on it." Mostly because Ethan had hoped his mother wouldn't press him into going, and now that he was married, he didn't have to. He doubted Catherine would want to go since she usually either kept to herself or had her father arrange dance partners for her. "I probably won't go."

"That's a shame. You seem to know which lady and gentleman go best together."

"No, I don't." Because if he did, he would've realized Catherine was good for him.

"You said Lord Roderick and his wife were a good match before anyone else saw it."

"What was to figure out about that one? She didn't tolerate his intimidating tactics. I saw the way she stood up to him that night everyone caught them out on Lady Cadwalader's lawn. He couldn't help but respect someone like that, and he couldn't love someone he didn't respect." Ethan wondered if Catherine's father left the townhouse yet. He took his watch out of his pocket and checked the time. Oh for goodness sakes! He wasn't a child. He could go to his townhouse any time he wanted. Tucking his watch back into his pocket, he rose to his feet. "All right. I think I'll go home and see what my wife is up to."

"Knowing you, you'll have no trouble entertaining her," Christopher replied with a wink.

Deciding to let Christopher's remark go unanswered, Ethan went to his townhouse. The first thing he did was check the drawing room, but Catherine wasn't there. He entertained the idea that she might be waiting for him in his bed but knew that was wishful thinking. She wouldn't be there until evening.

Turning to the butler who approached him, he asked, "Where's my wife?"

"She and the Duke of Rumsey left an hour ago. She said she'd return by early afternoon."

Ethan hid his disappointment. "Oh, well, that's good."

"A message came for you while you were gone. I put it in the library."

"Thank you."

Glad for something to do, he strode to the library and found the letter on his desk. It was from his acquaintance at Minerva Press. Since Catherine wouldn't return for a couple hours, he decided that he should deliver the letter to Agatha. She'd want to know what the publisher decided regarding her manuscript. Turning on his heel, he headed right back out of his townhouse.

Chapter Twelve

Catherine watched as the footman put the last of the new packages into the carriage. She knew her father felt guilty, but she had no idea he felt *this* guilty! Not only had he selected expensive fabric for two new dresses the seamstresses would make for her, but he'd also indulged her with jewelry, furs, and hats.

"I think this is enough," she told him, hoping by now his conscience was eased.

To her relief, he nodded. "I think that will do."

Good. As much as she appreciated all he was doing for her, she had no need for all the things he was buying her. She had more than enough from the last two Seasons when he blamed himself for not finding her a husband. And now he was blaming himself since she had one.

"Lady Edon," a familiar voice called out.

Ignoring the way her father winced at the mention of her title as Ethan's wife, Catherine looked over her shoulder and saw Claire with her sister. Pleased to see her new friend, Catherine smiled. "How do you do, Lady Roderick?"

"I'm very well. This is Mrs. Morris, my sister," she replied.

"I know who she is. It's a pleasure to meet you, Mrs. Morris."

Claire and her sister offered a greeting to the duke who reciprocated in kind. "It's a lovely day to be outside, isn't it?" Claire asked.

"Yes, it is," he replied.

Claire turned her attention back to Catherine. "We were on our way to Hyde Park." She motioned to the drawing pads in their hands. "We were going to draw some flowers. We have enough paper and pencils if you'd like to join us."

Excited by the prospect of spending the day with her friend, she looked at her father with a silent question in her eyes.

"I'll see to it that your things get to your home," her father said.

"Thank you," she replied, thrilled she'd get to spend time with other ladies who didn't have to be with her in order to be polite.

"If you need anything, tell me?" he asked.

"I will, and I'll be fine." She hoped that when she saw him again, he'd be happier.

He nodded, said good-bye to Claire and Mrs. Morris, and stepped into the carriage.

After the coachman urged the horses forward, Catherine turned back to the two ladies. "You said you're going to Hyde Park?"

"Yes. We could have taken a carriage, but it's such a nice day," Claire replied. "I hope you don't mind if we walk there."

"I don't mind at all. The day is perfect for a stroll. I've never drawn flowers at the park. In fact, I can't remember the last time I drew anything. I mainly painted pictures."

"You have no need to worry," Mrs. Morris said as they started walking down the sidewalk. "Neither Claire nor I are any good at drawing, and to be honest, I'm only doing it because she didn't want to go to Hyde Park alone."

"I was going to ask Catherine instead," Claire told her sister, "but given the fact that she just got married yesterday, I thought it was wise to let her adjust to her new life." She looked at Catherine. "How is your marriage so far?"

Though she blushed, Catherine said, "I think I'm going to like being married to Lord Edon."

"That's much better than how your marriage started," Mrs. Morris teased Claire and then turned her gaze to Catherine. "Claire's husband had to drag her out to their country estate, kicking and screaming the whole way."

"Well," Claire began, "you can't blame me. He accused me of all kinds of misdeeds. If he'd taken the time to listen to me, he would've known better. But that's the trouble with gentlemen. They don't often listen to a lady because their pride tells them they can't be wrong."

Catherine giggled.

"Some are more stubborn than others, but even so, you had an easier time with your husband than I had with mine, dear sister," Mrs. Morris said. "Mine wouldn't talk to me for nearly a month."

"Really? Why not?" Catherine asked, intrigued.

"I had to be creative in how I got him to marry me," she replied.

"She created a scandal to force his hand," Claire inserted.

Catherine's eyes grew wide. "You did?"

"Scandal is such a strong word," Mrs. Morris replied.

"Oh? And what would you call it?" Claire pressed.

"I'd call it encouragement." Mrs. Morris shrugged but grinned at Catherine. "Sometimes gentlemen need encouragement to do what's best for them."

"Tell me more about it," Catherine insisted, wondering what the lady had done to finally win her husband.

As they continued walking to the park, Mrs. Morris did as Catherine wished.

***

Ethan waited for Agatha at a bench at Hyde Park. She'd be dressed as Gilbert Horlock, which was her name as an author of gothic horror. In return for her submitting things to the *Tittletattle* on his behalf, he handled the correspondence between her and the publisher she hoped would accept her work.

He held the message from the publisher in his hand. He hadn't read it. He thought of slipping into her townhouse as he'd done when he sought her help with creating scandals about him, but he opted for sending a note to her butler. He couldn't leave the publisher's message with her butler but had to deliver it in person. She'd be mortified if anyone knew her secret, so her servants were the last people she'd reveal it to.

But since he had things to hide, he was safe. And likewise, she was safe to reveal his secrets to. And now Catherine knew the darkest secret he'd kept carefully concealed. She knew he wasn't the rake he pretended to be. And she accepted him anyway. He wondered if she welcomed it. Her attitude seemed to change right after she learned the truth.

"You have something for me?"

Looking up from where he sat on the bench, he saw Agatha dressed as Gilbert. Though she dressed the part of a young gentleman with a mustache, she used her real voice, keeping it low enough so no one passing by would overhear her.

He moved aside on the bench and motioned for her to sit. As she did, he said, "I do. The editor sent you a message." He presented the letter to her and she accepted it.

She took a deep breath. "I don't know if I should read this." She offered a light chuckle and turned the letter over in her hands.

"Do you want me to read it for you and tell you what he wrote?"

A long moment of silence passed before she answered. "No. I need to do it."

He watched as she read it, and as soon as he saw her wince, he knew the editor had rejected the story she submitted to him. Leaning toward her, he whispered, "I'm sorry."

She let out a shaky breath and wiped her eyes. After blinking a few times, she cleared her throat. "That's the third one he didn't want. Maybe I should stop writing."

"I don't think you can. You enjoy it too much."

"But what's the use? I can't share anything I've written with anyone. My family would be humiliated if they knew I wrote gothic horror, so I can't even share it with them, or even mention I write it."

"What's wrong with gothic horror?"

"They say it's a genre for the uneducated." She sighed. "I tire of hearing it."

"Let me read it."

"You don't care for gothic horror."

"How do you know?"

Her eyebrows rose. "Because the only books you've discussed actually enjoying are anything by William Shakespeare, Sophocles or Aesop. True, you enjoy fiction, but nothing you read involves a helpless heroine and a hero who saves her from certain danger."

"Just because I haven't read it yet doesn't mean I won't enjoy it. Give me a chance to decide for myself whether I like it or not."

"Even if I said yes, when will you find time? Isn't your wife keeping you occupied?"

"My wife is shopping with her father."

"Shopping?" She hesitated but shrugged. "I suppose it's to be expected. Yours isn't a love match. She'd be eager to run back to the safe and familiar world her father represents."

He laughed. "You don't know as much as you think you do. She's not afraid of embracing her new life."

"Well, she can't be that excited about it if she left you in favor of shopping."

"I don't know why she went shopping with her father. He came over right before breakfast because he spent all night worried about her." As if her father had anything to worry about!

"That's sweet of him."

Ethan grimaced. "Sweet?"

"Yes. He cares deeply for his daughter's well being. Not every parent is that way."

He resisted the urge to inform her that the duke's way of caring for Catherine involved threatening his life. When he turned his gaze to a couple of ladies heading in their direction, he straightened in surprise. Catherine was with Lady Roderick and Mrs. Morris. He didn't realize Catherine had any friends. Every time he'd seen her, she'd been either at her father's side, alone, or dancing with a gentleman her father matched her up with.

He glanced at Agatha. "Have you met Lady Catherine?"

"Isn't she Lady Edon now?" Agatha corrected, quickly stuffing the message into her pocket.

"Yes, I know. I just haven't gotten used to it yet." As they rose to their feet, he asked, "Have you met her?"

"No, and I hope she won't know who I really am."

He nodded, understanding the subtle request in her eyes. He wouldn't betray her trust by telling Catherine she was really Agatha, and besides, it wouldn't be appropriate if he'd been caught talking for so long with a lady he wasn't related or married to, especially when the lady in question was dressed as a gentleman. While he made it a habit of welcoming scandals in the past, he didn't relish one now—and it wasn't just because his father-in-law made it clear that scandals could be met with unfavorable consequences. He unconsciously rubbed his neck, recalling the way the edge of the smallsword felt pressed against its base. It was an experience he'd be very happy never repeating.

He waited for Catherine and her friends to come within hearing distance before he took a step forward to get Catherine's attention.

"My lord," Catherine said, her eyes wide, "I didn't realize you'd be here."

"Yes, well, I had a matter to tend to with a friend." He gestured to Agatha, praying Catherine and her friends would believe she was a gentleman. "This is Mr. Horlock."

Agatha bowed. "How do you do?" she asked in a deep voice.

Ethan ventured a look at Catherine and her friends to determine if they accepted Agatha's disguise. They offered their greetings in a manner that seemed to indicate they did.

"I see you have some drawing pads," Agatha said.

It was on the tip of Ethan's tongue to warn her to stop fiddling with her mustache since it appeared to be a little loose over her lip, but Lady Roderick answered, taking his mind off the mustache. "Since it's a lovely day, we thought we'd draw some flowers."

"Are you any good at it?" Agatha asked.

"I can't speak for my companions, but I wouldn't say drawing is my gift," Lady Roderick replied.

"She and I are horrid at it," Mrs. Morris added.

Agatha grinned, an action which made her mustache wobble a bit. "I appreciate a lady who is honest."

"And you?" Ethan asked Catherine. "Do you draw well?"

"I've had many lessons," Catherine replied. "It was something my father insisted on since my mother had a passion for it, though I mostly painted."

"But do you do it well?" Lady Roderick pressed.

She shrugged. "I don't know. I never showed anyone except my instructor and father my work, and while they said I did well, they might have been polite to spare my feelings."

"Then we'll have to see how you do and give you the truth either way," Mrs. Morris said. "We promise not to be brutal if they were wrong."

As the three ladies continued to talk, Ethan made eye contact with Agatha and motioned to his upper lip. Her eyes grew wide and she touched her mustache, her face growing red as she probably realized the thing was in danger of falling off.

To spare her potential embarrassment, Ethan waited for Lady Roderick to finish assuring Catherine couldn't draw worse than she did before he said, "It was a pleasure talking to you, but we must be off."

They turned their attention to him and Agatha as if surprised he spoke. Did they forget he and Agatha were there?

"Until we meet again," he continued with a quick bow. He would have lingered a bit longer since it was refreshing to see Catherine relaxed around other people, but Agatha caught her mustache as if fell off. Since her hand was clasped over her mouth, he said, "Now, Mr. Horlock, don't tell me that joke until we're out of the ladies' hearing."

As he led Agatha away from them, he caught sight of Catherine's wink and stopped for a moment. She then proceeded to turn to her friends and continued strolling down the path as if she hadn't done anything suggestive.

"Ethan," Agatha hissed. "Stop standing there with your tongue hanging out of your mouth."

Blinking, he turned his attention back to Agatha and hurried to catch up to her. "I didn't have my tongue hanging out of my mouth," he whispered.

"You were drooling."

"I was not."

She snorted. "Who would have thought it?"

Now he was starting to get irritated. "Who would have thought what?"

"That you would actually like your new life as a married gentleman?" Before he could refute her claim, she added, "I'll send you a message when my next story is ready for the publisher."

As she hurried down the street, he turned and headed for his townhouse.

Chapter Thirteen

$\mathcal{E}$than felt ridiculous as he paced back and forth in the drawing room. He should be in his library reading, or at least pretending he was reading one of his books. But if he was in the library, he might miss seeing Catherine when she came home. Who knew if she'd venture to his library again? He certainly hadn't minded it when she took him to it earlier. In fact, he hoped she'd do it again, but he'd never voice the thought. He was a gentleman, after all, and didn't want to upset her sensibilities.

With a snort, he turned on his heel and paced in the opposite direction. Upset her sensibilities? She came to his bed with the intention of making love, rubbed his thigh at the table while her father was in the room, and fondled him in the library. He doubted he could do anything to upset her sensibilities!

Footsteps approached the drawing room, so he rushed to the door in hopes that Catherine had finally come home. When he realized the footman had opened the door for his mother, he sighed in disappointment. "Oh, it's just you."

She arched an eyebrow as she entered the room. "It's a pleasure to see you, too, my dear son."

"I didn't mean it that way," he quickly amended. "Of course, I'm happy to see you."

"Of course, you are."

He ignored the sarcasm in her voice. "Have you been shopping today?"

"No. I decided to pay a friend a visit. With Catherine and her father gone, I had no one to talk to."

He nodded and turned on his heel to pace the room once more.

She frowned and followed him with her gaze. "What are you doing?"

"I thought I'd look around the room." He motioned absentmindedly to the things around them. "I haven't been in here for a while. There might be something we can add to make it more attractive."

With a smirk, she said, "Or you might be waiting for a certain young lady to come into the room to relax after a long day of shopping with her father."

He narrowed his eyes at her. "Catherine never once crossed my mind."

She clucked her tongue and shook her head. "Of all things, I didn't take you for a liar."

"If I lie, it's because I've had a good teacher."

She gasped and placed her hand to her chest. "Are you implying I have a tendency to lie?"

Raising his voice an octave, he clasped his hands together and imitated the smile she'd used the night of the Duke of Rumsey's ball. "Your Grace, it wouldn't be fair to deny true love. My son and your daughter are meant for each other."

"I did not screech like a harpy!" Though she placed her hands on her hips and glared at him in indignation, he caught the slight smile on her lips. She was struggling not to laugh.

In an effort to get her to break down and laugh, he added, "Everyone, and I mean every single person in London, knows of their secret engagement. It wouldn't do well to forbid these two marriage lest they succumb to suicide like poor Romeo and Juliet."

"I didn't say you and Catherine would commit suicide," she corrected, giggling.

"It was implied." Forcing aside his urge to chuckle, he added in a higher voice, "I know what's best for you, Ethan. Now stay here while I arrange the rest of your life for you." He caught a movement out of the corner of his eye, so he turned in time to see Catherine standing in the doorway, her eyebrows raised in interest and a drawing pad in her arms. Heat rose to his face and he cleared his throat. "Did you enjoy your time at the park?" he asked as if he hadn't been caught imitating his mother.

"I dare say I didn't enjoy my afternoon as much as you," Catherine replied.

He straightened his waistcoat and glanced at his mother who gave a slight shrug. Smiling, he walked over to Catherine. "May I see what you drew?"

To his surprise, she clutched the drawing pad to her chest. "It's just flowers. A bunch of them."

"Oh, I love flowers!" his mother exclaimed.

His mother headed in her direction, but Catherine took a step back and gave a tentative laugh. "They're boring, I assure you. In fact, they're not even good. You can't even tell they're flowers. I think I'll take them to my bedchamber." Before they could respond, she whirled around and scurried off.

Ethan turned to his mother.

"Don't ask me," she replied. "I have no idea what all that was about. Well, I'm going to change for dinner."

She left the room, and after a moment, he decided to change for dinner, too.

***

Unfortunately, Catherine wasn't sitting next to Ethan during dinner. He told himself this was a good thing. He didn't need her touching his thigh and distracting him from his meal. Even though his body wanted nothing more than to feel her hands on it, he kept telling himself he was better off focusing on his meal. He could barely eat during breakfast, and it wasn't just because the duke watched him. So yes, he was far better off with her sitting safely across from him.

He did wonder why she hadn't bothered coming to his bedchamber before dinner. He fully expected her to pop in and seduce him like she had in the library, but she didn't. Not that he was disappointed. He wasn't. He was merely surprised since she made it a point to approach him intimately earlier that day.

"It's a shame you didn't get a chance to go to Hyde Park together," his mother rambled as he ate the fish on his plate.

"We saw each other at Hyde Park," Catherine said after she took a sip of wine.

"You did?" His mother glanced between them.

"Yes, we did. I went to draw with Lady Roderick and Mrs. Morris, and he was there with another gentleman."

Ethan noticed the relief that flickered across his mother's face and knew it was because his mother was glad he'd been caught talking to a gentleman instead of dallying with a lady. "I wish you'd show us what you drew," Ethan told Catherine.

Catherine's cheeks turned a pretty shade of pink that flattered her complexion. "They're only flowers, and like I said earlier, they aren't very good." She brushed a reddish curl behind her ear and shifted in her chair.

He couldn't be sure, but he sensed her apprehension and wondered what it was about the flowers she drew that made her nervous.

"I don't recall seeing Mr. Horlock before," Catherine continued as she poked her fish with her fork. "Is he new to London?"

It took him a moment to realize she was talking about Agatha. "Oh, yes. I did meet with him today." He glanced at his mother. "I was talking to him when Catherine and her friends came by with their drawing pads."

"Mr. Horlock?" his mother asked. "I don't recall hearing you mention a Mr. Horlock before."

"I rarely associate with him, so I wouldn't have mentioned him," he replied, taking another bite of his fish.

"I don't recall hearing anything about him either," Catherine added, "and my father knew all the bachelors so he could—" She stopped and lowered her gaze to her plate.

She didn't need to finish the sentence. Her father made it a point to know all the bachelors in London in order to find a good husband for her. Hoping to ease her embarrassment over how difficult it'd been for her to secure a husband, he opted to get the topic back to Agatha's facade. "Well, Mr. Horlock has no interest in social affairs. In fact, he's a recluse."

"If that's true, then what was he doing at Hyde Park?" his mother asked.

He resisted the urge to sigh. Leave it to his mother to inquire further into an issue than necessary. "I don't make it a habit to ask why gentlemen do what they do, Mother."

She swallowed a piece of her fish and furrowed her eyebrows. "It doesn't make any sense. Did you go to his house and take him to the park?"

"No. We happened to meet there." Goodness, like he had to escort a gentleman to the park!

"But you just said he doesn't like going outside."

"I didn't say he doesn't like going outside."

"Of course, you did," she insisted. "You said he was a recluse."

"That doesn't mean he doesn't enjoy going out when it's nice outside."

She shook her head. "I fail to believe it, Ethan. Either he's a recluse or he isn't. Hyde Park is full of people. Why, you and Catherine were there, and you weren't even expecting to see each other. And she was with two friends. Why would a recluse want to go to a place where many people go?"

This time he groaned and let her see how exasperated he was. "Good heavens, Mother, you'll keep on about this till the break of dawn if I let you. Just because Mr. Horlock went for a walk, it doesn't mean he wanted to engage in a conversation with anyone."

"But he was talking to you."

He let the fork fall to the table and put his face in his hands.

Across from him, Catherine giggled. "I think he might mean that Mr. Horlock is a recluse when it comes to the fairer sex. When I met him, he seemed horribly shy. He covered his mouth as if he was afraid we'd think whatever he had to say was silly, and he ran off in a hurry."

Ethan looked up at Catherine.

She picked up her glass of wine. "Lady Roderick, Mrs. Morris, and I agreed that he was the oddest gentlemen we'd ever met. Now I can tell them why."

Ethan was ready to tell her she would do no such thing since it would make Agatha seem foolish, but then he reasoned it was better than them finding out Agatha was a lady dressed as a gentleman. One could hardly tarnish the reputation of someone who didn't exist anyway.

His mother shrugged and resumed eating her meal.

"What did you do today, Mother?" he finally asked.

To his relief she forgot all about Mr. Horlock and began a long spiel about her afternoon. He was able to finish his main course and dessert without any more awkward questions. He hardly paid attention to what his mother said. She was discussing the beautiful parlor of her friend at great length, and such talk had a tendency to make him sleepy well before bedtime.

But on this particular evening, he had Catherine to watch. Though Catherine did a much better job of keeping up with everything his mother was saying, she would glance at him from time to time and give him a suggestive look that sent a jolt of heat straight to his loins. There was no doubt about it. He had to get her up to her bedchamber and soon. He'd spent the entire day in agony, and his patience had come to an end. As soon as dinner was over, he encouraged his mother to tend to her needlework and escorted Catherine upstairs.

Chapter Fourteen

"*I* thought we were going to your bed," Catherine said as he opened the door to her bedchamber and stepped inside.

It wasn't his intention to be rude by going into her room first, but he knew it was his only advantage to finding that drawing pad. He didn't think she would hide it since she planned to go to his bedchamber that evening. The first thing he did was go to the table and light several candles, careful to keep an eye on his wife who was now in the room.

He lifted one of the candles and turned to get a better view of the room. The onslaught of peach, ruffles, and lace nearly assaulted his senses. The color wasn't so bad, but he wondered if he could maintain an erection surrounded by such frivolous ruffles and lace.

She closed the door and faced him, looking at him with big, trusting eyes, her hands folded in front of her. "Are you all right?"

He blinked and shook his head, willing the mountain of frilly material from his mind. He came here to find out what made her so squeamish about the flowers she drew, and he wasn't leaving this room until he found that drawing pad! Taking a deep breath, he strengthened his resolve.

"I'm fine," he replied, sidestepping the bed, making sure he didn't brush against the side of the canopy.

He'd never been to this room, and now he knew why. His mother probably arranged this room to look this way to torment him. No. That didn't make sense. She wanted him to get an heir. The truth was, she wasn't thinking at all when she ordered the bedding. He hadn't noticed the rugs before, but they were as excessive as the bedding. White, fluffy rugs. The whole place smelled of flowers, so he scanned the tables and saw vases strategically placed all over the room. There was no way a gentleman could make love in this situation. He would have to take Catherine back to his bedchamber…after he found the drawing pad.

"Ethan, where are you going?" Catherine asked as he headed for the small room off to the side of her bedchamber.

"Oh, I just want to make sure you're comfortable." He glanced behind him where she stood by the bed. She looked so tiny compared to the pile of blankets and ruffled pillows. "You don't have to keep this room the way it is. My mother has a tendency to get…excited," that was putting it mildly, "so I understand if you want to decorate this room another way."

She looked around the room. "I like it."

"You do?" He stopped himself before he said anything about his mother's horrible taste. If Catherine liked things the way they were, she wouldn't be pleased if he voiced his opinion because she might construe that as his opinion of her—and that wasn't the case.

"Yes. It's very pretty," she replied, smiling at him.

He offered a nod and turned his attention to the desk in the other room.

"What are you doing?" she asked as he walked over to it.

"Oh, just seeing if there's anything I should buy for you," he mumbled as he walked around the desk.

The drawing pad wasn't on top of it. Maybe it was in a drawer. He pulled open one of the drawers. No. Not in there.

He opened another one. Not there either. As he opened the third drawer, he noticed she was standing in the doorway.

"Good. You have plenty of stationary. I wanted to be sure you have everything you need." He ventured a good look at her. Did she believe him?

If she didn't believe him, she didn't give any indication about it. Instead, her smile widened. "It's very kind of you to worry about me."

"Yes, I suppose it is." He opened the last three drawers and sighed in disappointment. The drawing pad wasn't in any of them. Where could it be?

"While I appreciate it, wouldn't you rather be doing something else?" she asked and stepped toward him.

He moved to the other side of the desk and hurried back to the large room. If he wasn't quick, she'd figure out what he was doing and his chance to find the drawing pad would be lost. "I thought your lady's maid would help you..." he cleared his throat and dodged her when she reached for him... "undress."

With a teasing grin, she asked, "Wouldn't you rather do it?"

He offered a weak laugh and scanned the room. Where would she put a drawing pad? The thing wasn't exactly small. It should be easy to find unless she put it somewhere no one would expect. On a whim, he bent forward and checked under the chairs in the room. But he didn't find it.

To his surprise, she approached him from behind and wrapped her arms around his waist. He let out a startled shriek and almost dropped the candle.

"You really shouldn't scare a person like that," he said, his heart racing.

She walked around to face him and hugged him. "I'm so glad you're not the rake I thought you were!"

He struggled to keep the candle steady in its holder. "Uh, Catherine. The candle."

"Oh, I'm sorry." She pulled away from him and took the candle so she could set it on the table by her bed. "I know it's not typical for a gentleman to come into his marriage untouched by a lady, but it greatly pleases me that you did."

"Why?" Wouldn't a lady prefer a gentleman who knew what he was doing?

"Because it's something we get to experience for the first time together."

Though he didn't see the importance of it, he offered an obligatory nod and tried to determine where else he could look for a drawing pad.

"Maybe it's silly, but I did so few things with others while growing up. I always wanted to do something special with someone that they'd never done with anyone else."

His gaze traced the furniture by her gaudy bed, the vanity table, and the armoire.

"Ethan?"

"Hmm…?" He narrowed his eyes as something on top of the armoire caught his attention.

"Are you listening to me?"

"Of course I am," he lied, turning his gaze to her. He patted her on the shoulder and smiled. "And I agree."

She furrowed her eyebrows. "You agree?"

"Sure. What you said is right." Whatever that something was… By the disappointed look on her face, it suddenly occurred to him that he was too hasty to say he agreed with her. He assumed she'd asked him a question, but apparently, that hadn't been the case. "You really won't show me what you drew today?"

She gasped, her eyes wide. "You came here because you wanted to see my drawings? You didn't want to be with me?"

"That's nonsense. I want to be with you." Now that was true. He'd thought of nothing but being with her all day.

"Then why are you searching my room for a drawing pad instead of undressing me?"

Unfortunately, that was an excellent question. It was just his luck that he ended up marrying a lady who wasn't a dullard. However, inspiration struck. "I've never removed a lady's clothes in my entire life. I wouldn't know what to do."

Her frown deepened.

"I'm being honest. Tell me, Catherine, do you feel comfortable undressing me?"

"You're trying to avoid answering my question."

"I am not. We're talking about undressing, and I made a valid point."

She placed her hands on her hips and scanned him up and down. "Fine. I'll take the challenge." She reached up and started unbuttoning his waistcoat.

Startled, he stepped back. He hadn't expected her to actually do it! Well, that only proved that he couldn't depend on her to show a smidgen of the shyness virgins were supposedly known for.

"I thought you wanted me to undress you," she said, frustration in her voice. "I don't understand you at all. Earlier today, you seemed more than ready to be in bed with me."

"You're the one who accosted me."

"Accosted?"

"Yes. First, you barge into my bedchamber and demand I consummate the marriage. Second, you stroked my thigh at breakfast—with your father right there might I add. Third, you fondle me in the library. And now you're trying to rip my clothes off. Really, I'm beginning to think I'm nothing but an amusement to you."

She stared at him for a moment. "I was under the impression that gentlemen liked bedroom activities."

"Where did you get that idea?"

"Your reputation as a rake, for one, indicated you frequently took ladies off to somewhere private to engage in such deeds. I don't have to know everything about it to get the general idea of what gentlemen want."

He shrugged. "While it's true that gentlemen are interested in the bedchamber, sometimes it's nice to be appreciated for who we are. I happen to have hopes, desires, feelings..." His gaze drifted back to the drawing pad. *And a healthy amount of curiosity.*

"Well, then perhaps ladies might also have the urge to participate in bedroom activities. Why, just this morning, I discovered something about myself that I never knew possible, and I'd like to experience it with you. But it seems that you have no interest in me at all."

Noting the hurt tone in her voice, he turned his attention back to her. "That's not true. You're surprisingly interesting."

"You're just saying that to make me feel better." She went to a drawer on her bedside table and opened it. After she pulled out a handkerchief, she wiped her eyes.

Oh goodness! She wasn't going to cry in front of him, was she? He had no idea what to do with a weeping female. Indeed, such a situation terrified him. He hurried over to her and took the handkerchief from her. "There's no reason to cry. I mean it. You intrigue me. More than I expected when our marriage was arranged. I admit I thought you'd bore a gentleman to tears—"

She huffed, her cheeks a bright shade of pink and her expression hard.

He dropped the handkerchief on the table and took her hands in his. "The truth is, you're a very exciting lady."

Her face softened. "You think so?"

"You're lively and passionate. You're the most wonderful person I've ever met. I'm pleased to find out how wrong I was— how wrong we all were. I should thank you for putting on the pretense you did. I'm glad you didn't end up with someone else before my mother meddled in our lives."

A smile spread across her lips, lighting her entire face.

"You are so beautiful when you smile," he whispered.

Then, because it seemed to be the appropriate thing to do, he bowed his head and kissed her. In no hurry to end the kiss, he took his time to savor the moment, exploring her mouth with his tongue, noting the way she responded to him. His body, which had suffered all day long for this moment, prompted him to try his hand at undressing her.

He wanted to see her bare flesh again. The memory of her pink nipples surrounded by soft white mounds and the patch of reddish curls between her legs made him forget all about the drawing pad. He found that the garishly feminine room didn't even bother him at the moment. His only focus was now on her and how much he wanted to pursue the more sensual side of their marriage.

He wanted to be as suave as other gentlemen probably were when it came to the task of undressing their wives, but he found himself fumbling a few times, especially when it came to undoing her corset. The row of buttons down her back were so small, he had to squint in the candlelight to find them all, and the strings on her corset weren't as easy to loosen as they should have been. Her shift, mercifully, was easy since all he had to do was pull it over her head. He managed to get a full view of her before she started to remove his clothes.

He was too aroused to notice if she struggled with removing his clothes or not. Her breasts brushed his body and her hands brushed his erection in ways that made him sigh in anticipation of what was to come. Tonight, he wouldn't give thought to her father because doing so would only delay their lovemaking further, and there was no way his body would forgive him for that.

He pulled back the covers on her bed before he picked her up in his arms and laid her down. He settled next to her and embraced her, relishing the feel of her soft curves as they pressed against him. She was just as wonderful as he remembered from the previous night. He ran his hands over her body. She didn't seem to mind. In fact, she squirmed and moaned in a way that let him know she was enjoying it. Even better than that, she was exploring him with the same passion he was exploring her.

At one point, he brought his mouth to her breast, pleased when she ran her fingers through his hair and gently encouraged him to linger there. He teased and licked her nipple, satisfied when she shivered in pleasure beneath him. So this nipple was sensitive. Curious, he explored her other breast with his tongue and suckled it, noting that the other nipple was just as sensitive.

"Ethan," she whispered, her breathing raspy, "touch me here while you do that."

She brought his hand between her legs and guided two of his fingers into her while centering his thumb on her sensitive nub. Keeping her hand over his, she instructed him on how to best bring her pleasure. It excited him that she didn't hesitate to let him know what she wanted. She wasn't shy at all about insisting he bring her pleasure, and after what he'd learned about the temptress beneath her cool exterior, he wanted nothing more than to find out what she would do when she finally had her release.

He stroked her core, aware of the way her warm, moist flesh tightened around him as he rubbed her nub. Mindful of her sensitive nipples, he continued his gentle assault on them, nipping and licking them. Her moans came louder, further exciting him. When she reached her peak, she cried out and grasped his shoulders, digging her nails into them. He lifted his head and watched her expression. So this was how a lady looked when she was at the height of sensual pleasure. It seemed to be a mixture of pleasure and pain, something hard to pinpoint but something he wanted to see every time they were in bed.

When he was assured she was done, he rolled on top of her and entered her. This time there was no barrier he had to press through and no gasp of surprise from her to indicate he'd hurt her. She lifted her hips to better accommodate him and murmured for him to press deeper into her. He didn't need further encouragement. He moved inside her, groaning as her flesh squeezed him. It felt so heavenly. Despite his desire to take his time, the day of longing for this moment was too much for him. He managed several thrusts before he released his seed, his body shuddering above her in response. Afterwards, he collapsed in her arms, out of breath and blissfully sated. This had to be the best experience in the world.

When his head cleared, he kissed her then grabbed the bed covers so they wouldn't get chilly during the night. She sighed in contentment and snuggled up to him. He brought his arms around her and kissed the top of her head before resting his cheek on it. The lack of sleep the previous night was quickly catching up to him, and before he knew it, he fell into a very satisfying sleep.

Chapter Fifteen

*C*atherine woke in the middle of the night and glanced at the top of her armoire. How was she to know Ethan would look up there? And how was she to know he wanted to look at her drawing pad so much? Her face warmed when she thought of the drawings she'd etched. If she'd shown him the two pictures she'd drawn of the flowers, she knew he'd want to see the rest of her drawings, and she'd die of mortification if he saw the others. Claire and her sister didn't ask to see more than the flowers, as she knew they wouldn't.

But flowers were only so interesting for so long. She'd looked at flowers her entire life. While Claire and her sister could draw them for hours, Catherine found she needed something more fascinating to draw. So she drew the only thing that held her interest. And there was no way she'd let Ethan see that she'd been drawing him…without clothes. Quite frankly, she didn't think he'd appreciate it, mostly because he might assume she'd shown it to her new friends.

Of course, she hadn't. Such a thing wouldn't have been ladylike at all, especially since he was her husband. Now that she knew no other lady had seen him naked, she rather enjoyed the secret in knowing only she had. And besides, she didn't think respectable ladies spent their time drawing a naked man. It seemed that they were more likely to study flowers and other such nonsense.

Next to her, Ethan let out a contented sigh and rolled to his back. He'd left the candles lit, so she had a good view of the armoire. Her gaze traveled to the top of it. She had to get it down from there before he woke up. She'd rip out the two pages she'd drawn of him and burn them. Then she'd show him the flowers and he'd leave her alone about it.

When she was assured he was asleep, she slipped away from him, careful so that the mattress didn't shake too much. She managed to get out of bed without incident. A slight chill in the room sent goosebumps along her bare skin, but she didn't pay them any mind. She tiptoed to a chair in the corner of the room and carried it over to the armoire.

Ethan mumbled, and she immediately stilled. After a few agonizing seconds passed, she ventured a look in his direction and saw him roll onto his side so that his back was to her. Breathing a sigh of relief, she set the chair down on the rug, thankful it didn't make a sound. She stood up on the chair and retrieved the drawing pad. With another glance at him to make sure he was still asleep, she descended from the chair.

She tucked the pad under her arm and carried her chair back to where it originally was. Biting her lower lip, she tried to decide where a good hiding place would be. She needed somewhere large enough to hold the pad. Drumming her fingers on the pad, she studied the room. He had an aversion to ruffles and lace and overtly feminine colors. She'd never forget the look of horror on his face when he saw her bed sheets and canopy. She stifled back a giggle and decided she'd be better off hiding it in something that would offend his masculinity.

She quietly slipped it under her side of the foot of the bed. She gathered enough of the cloth from her canopy to go around the leg of the bed, assured he wouldn't touch the material to expose the drawing pad. While he could make love in the bed, she expected he only did so because the male part of him convinced him he could touch the sheets as long as he was touching her, too. But if there was no incentive for him to spend time near the bed, she knew he wouldn't do it. So if he snuck into her room while she wasn't there, he wouldn't dare go near the bed.

Satisfied, she returned to Ethan, careful as she slid under the covers. True, the bedding was frilly and extravagant, but she secretly liked it this way. Ethan rolled onto his back again and murmured something about fencing. What a strange thing to mention, she thought. Did all gentlemen dream of sporting? He'd made reference to fencing the night before as well. Shrugging, she settled next to him. It might be that she'd never understand her husband, but really, that was all right.

His eyelids fluttered open and his eyes focused on her in the candlelight.

She smiled and snuggled up to him. "You're awake."

He shivered and put his arms around her. "And you're cold."

"That's because I need you to warm me up."

Returning her smile, he kissed her. And in due time, they were making love again.

***

"Is something troubling you?" Catherine asked Ethan as they ate breakfast the next morning.

"No, nothing's wrong," he quickly assured her, offering a smile in hopes she'd believe his lie.

To his relief, she nodded and turned her attention back to his mother. He wasn't sure what the two ladies were talking about. He thought someone said something about a dress, but he tuned most of their conversation out. They were discussing idle lady things, and he had better things to do than dwell on such matters.

What confounded him on this particular morning was the blasted drawing pad. He knew he saw it on top of the armoire, and yet, when he woke up that morning, it was gone. It was as if the thing had vanished into thin air. Such a thing was impossible, he knew. Catherine must have gotten up at some point in the night and hid it somewhere else. That explained why her skin was so chilly last night when he woke from his sleep.

For a moment, his mind went back to the peculiar dream he'd been having. He was fencing with someone he assumed to be her father, but when it came time to take off their masks, he realized it was her. She proceeded to take off all of her clothes then announced they would fence in the nude.

He woke up at that point, fully erect and desiring to claim her as his wife once more. He'd been so excited she was awake and willing that he hadn't bothered to think of the drawing pad. But when he woke up that morning, the pad was gone, and he had no idea where she put it. Of course now that they were at breakfast in front of his mother, he couldn't ask her about it.

No. He'd have to wait. Perhaps he could convince her to show it to him if he was sweet enough. She seemed to respond well when he complimented her. There was plenty to compliment her about, and the more he got to know her, the more delightful she was becoming.

"What will you be doing today?" his mother asked after she finished her fruit.

Since she was looking at him, Ethan decided to answer. "It depends."

"On what?"

"On whether or not the Duke of Terror comes to make sure Catherine is still alive and well."

As he hoped, Catherine laughed at his joke. "The Duke of Terror? Is that how you view my father?"

"Naturally. The gentleman is a formidable wall of terror."

His mother rolled her eyes but grinned.

Catherine laughed harder and pressed her hand to her chest. "Oh, he is not. He's harmless."

"You haven't fenced with him," he replied.

"Is that why you keep mumbling something about fencing while you sleep?" She gasped and glanced around the room. "My apologies," she whispered. "I shouldn't have been so quick to speak."

"It's good you did," his mother said. "It assures me he's doing his duty to get an heir. His father would be relieved. Maybe he's watching from Heaven and is rejoicing that the title will pass on to his grandson."

"There's no need to exaggerate the matter, Mother," he admonished, though mention of an heir didn't irk him as much as it usually would. Even if she was obsessed with him producing one, he could at least rest in knowing that now there was a possibility. And truth be told, he wouldn't mind many more tries at getting that heir. Forcing his mind back to his mother, he added, "Besides, Catherine might have all girls. You can't take it for granted she'll have a boy." He glanced at his wife. "Whichever one you have is fine with me. I don't hold so tenaciously to the title as most gentlemen do."

Leaning closer to him in interest, she asked, "Why is that?"

"I suppose it's because I've seen enough gentlemen who assume a title gives them the right to treat others with disdain. I didn't feel sorry for half the gentlemen who lost their money to me in those gambling hells."

His mother drew in a sharp breath. "Ethan!"

"It's the truth. You'd be horrified to know some of the things I learned." These were things he'd never tell her, though he could tell by Catherine's raised eyebrows that her curiosity was at war with her sensibilities. "Suffice it to say that some gentlemen aren't what they seem."

Catherine bit her lower lip and glanced at his mother. He knew it was on the tip of her tongue to press him for a story or two but didn't dare reveal her desire to hear such gossip while his mother was nearby. Maybe he could convince her to show him some of her drawings in exchange for some tales. He wouldn't tell her the worst of it, of course. She was a lady, and even if she had some strong passions, he still needed to protect her from some of the harsher realities of life.

"I won't torment you with details," Ethan assured his mother who looked relieved.

Catherine seemed disappointed but didn't protest.

"Catherine, is there anything you wish to do today in the unlikely event your father won't be stopping by?" he asked.

"I wouldn't mind seeing a circus," she replied with a hopeful expression that made her look completely adorable. "My father never let me go there. I'm not sure why."

Who knew she'd taken an interest in the circus? He couldn't even begin to guess why the duke didn't let her go to one. However, he had no qualms about taking her there. "We'll go. Even if the Duke of Terror shows up, we'll tell him to come back at a more convenient time."

His mother shot him a stern look. "You mustn't refer to him that way anymore. What if you slip and call him that when he's around?"

"He would love nothing more than to send me to an early grave," Ethan told her. "If I do slip, it shouldn't surprise him."

Though Catherine giggled, she argued, "My father isn't as terrible as you make him out to be. Now, you said you'd take me to the circus?"

Her eyes grew wide in the most charming fashion, and he honestly didn't think he could deny her anything when she looked at him that way. In some ways, she seemed so innocent. No one would believe she was capable of such passion. He ventured that she also had a tendency to be fiercely loyal to those she loved.

And he also ventured that he was a very fortunate gentleman to have married her.

His mind turning back to her inquiry, he nodded. "Yes. We'll go to the circus."

She clasped her hands together. "Splendid! I'll get dressed in appropriate clothes."

As she stood, he touched her arm to stop her. "There's no need. We won't be going for a couple of hours."

After a moment's hesitation, she sighed. "I'll go restless if I wait."

"I'll tell you what. I'll change clothes as well, and we can take a stroll before the circus starts."

His mother smiled in a way that indicated she was pleased with his response, but he chose to ignore it. He didn't need his mother getting sentimental in front of the servants. "What will you be doing today, Mother?" he asked before he finished his milk.

"I'll pay someone a visit," she replied. "You don't have to worry about me."

He narrowed his eyes at her. He debated whether or not he should ask her who she intended to visit but decided against it. She was a grown lady. He hadn't made it a habit of keeping track of her whereabouts in the past, and he saw no reason to start now. As they rose from the table, he told her, "I hope you have a good day."

"I will." With a twinkle in her eye, she added in a low voice, "I'm happy that you will be doing something suitable for a change."

Resisting the urge to groan, he followed Catherine to the hallway, for once glad that someone knew he wasn't the rake he had pretended to be. He used to think that someone finding out his secret would be the worst thing that could happen to him. But in a way, it proved to be the exact opposite. Catherine knew his secret but would never tell anyone, which made him feel at ease.

More than that, however, was knowing he didn't have to put on a pretense with her. He could be the gentleman he truly was when she was around, and that felt more liberating than losing his title would have been. With her, he could be himself. And with him, he sensed that she could put aside the show of being a proper young lady and explore more of her true self as well.

It was ironic when he thought about it. Here he was, far more reserved than he let others believe while she was far more passionate than others would have thought her to be. They were an odd pair, really. But even as odd as they were, he suspected they would also be a happy one.

Chapter Sixteen

"What a delightful day it's been!" Catherine exclaimed as the carriage pulled up to the townhouse.

Ethan grinned. "I thought you'd enjoy the circus."

"I did. I enjoyed it immensely! Thank you for taking me."

"I'll take you anywhere your heart desires. Just tell me where you want to go, and we'll go there."

She kissed his cheek. "That's very kind of you."

The footman opened the door, and they left the carriage. He waited until they were alone in the entryway before he decided it was time to ask about her drawing pad.

"Will you be getting changed for dinner?" he asked, glancing at the stairs leading to her bedchamber.

"I was thinking of it," she replied and headed for the staircase.

Good. That made things easier for him. "I should get dressed for dinner as well." He ran to catch up to her and joined her as she walked up the steps. "Is there anything you need help with?"

"My lady's maid helps me when I change clothes."

"Wouldn't it be more fun if I helped you instead?"

She paused and studied him. "Well, it would, but there's a difference between taking clothes off and putting them on, especially when you're dealing with corsets and gowns."

"Oh, I was thinking I'd help you out of your dress, not put the next one on."

Her lips curled up into a wicked grin. "Dare we in the middle of the day?"

He shrugged. "Why not? Is there a law that says we can't spend time in bed before dinner?"

"No, at least not that I know of."

"So?"

They reached the top of the steps and she turned to face him. "Considering how much I enjoyed last night, I'd be foolish to say no."

He followed her down the hall, and when he realized she was heading for his bedchamber, he called out, "I was thinking we could go to your room."

"I thought after your reaction to seeing my room last night, it'd be best to go to yours. I don't want there to be any problems with," she motioned to his crotch, "it."

Understanding her meaning, he laughed. "I was able to perform last night. Twice, in fact."

"That's true, but I wanted to make sure you could perform again given that it's daylight and the curtains are parted so you can see every overtly feminine thing in the room."

He put his arm around her waist and pulled her toward him. "I think you'll manage to make sure I don't have any problems."

He bowed his head and kissed her. When the kiss ended, she looked up at him with an innocent expression that seemed to border on seduction.

"If you're sure..." she whispered, her hand tracing his erection.

He let out a playful growl and led her to her bedchamber.

She giggled. "There might be a part in you that's a rake after all," she said in a low voice.

"Only with you."

Glad she opened the door to her bedchamber, he followed her into her room and scanned the area. Well, at least the peach bedding didn't make him shiver this time. He was getting used to it.

Hoping he sounded barely interested, he ventured, "Why don't you showcase any of your drawings?"

"Why would I do that?" she asked as she shut the door and turned to him.

"Because you'd like to see what you created?"

"Even if it's not that good?"

"It's your bedchamber. Who cares if you're any good or not?"

"I care," she replied as she went over to him and wrapped her arms around his waist.

Though she kissed his neck in a way that further aroused him, he pressed forward. "What can I do to persuade you to let me see your drawings? Should I tell you some secrets I learned about a couple of gentlemen that my mother didn't want me to say during breakfast?"

She shook her head. "I was tempted to hear more, but I think I better not. There are some things I think I'm better off not knowing."

Drat! That was the only thing he had to bargain with.

"You really want to see my drawings?" she asked.

He studied her expression to see if she was trying to bait him, but she seemed sincere. "Yes, I would. I'd like to see if you have a talent for it." And he wanted to see what she'd be so shy about.

"All right. I'll show you, but you must close your eyes so you won't find my hiding place."

His wife really had him intrigued. Who knew she had such a mischievous side to her? "Why? What else are you hiding from me?"

"A lady can't reveal all her secrets." She winked at him before adding, "Now, turn away from me and close your eyes. Then I'll get it."

He obeyed, and he heard her moving around the room. He was tempted to glance over his shoulder and see where she'd made her hiding place but decided, just this once, he'd be good and not peek.

"You can look now," she said as she came around him so she was standing in front of him.

Opening his eyes, he saw the drawing pad she held out to him. "Are you sure about this?" he asked as he took it. "You seemed hesitant yesterday."

"I know. It was silly, but I didn't think you'd like my flowers."

He turned his attention to the drawing pad. She appeared much too eager for him to look at it, didn't she? Was it possible that it was simple nerves that made her hesitate so? He glanced at her and thought of how bold she'd been in the short time he'd been married to her. For some reason, she didn't strike him as the type of lady who would mind showing anyone pictures of flowers. He flipped through the drawing pad and saw two drawings. One with a group of flowers together and another with a single flower.

"These are good," he commented, flipping through the rest of the pad to see if there was another drawing—perhaps something less innocent—hidden somewhere.

"You really think so?" she asked, circling around him so she could see the drawings.

"Yes. Exquisite work, in fact. Some would say these flower look lifelike. Did you show these to Lady Roderick and Mrs. Morris?"

"Yes, I did."

And she was hesitant to show these to him? That was even stranger. "What did they say when they saw them?"

"The same thing you did."

"So why didn't you want me to see them?"

With a giggle that had a slight unease to it, she shrugged. "You're a gentleman. I didn't think flowers would interest you."

He took another good look at her drawings. There were only two. While she managed to capture every detail with surprising clarity, he thought she could've drawn more in the time she'd been at Hyde Park. Well, there was no way to prove if there had been something else in this pad, maybe something she'd removed to save herself some embarrassment.

"You have nothing to worry about," he said as he closed it and handed it to her. "Your drawings are wonderful. Why don't you showcase them in the drawing room?"

"There are already paintings gracing the walls." She set the pad on the settee by the window then returned to him. "I believe we came here to do something more interesting than look at flowers."

At least there was that. Even if seeing the drawing pad was a disappointment, he could enjoy the rest of his time before dinner. With a grin, he took her in his arms and carried her to the bed where he proceeded to make love to her.

Chapter Seventeen

A month later, Ethan and Catherine were at Hyde Park. The sun warmed the cool spring air, making it a pleasant day. The scent of flowers floated on the breeze. The birds sung their sweet melodies. It was an ideal day to be at the park. A perfect day, really. But still, he felt foolish sitting still while Catherine drew his profile. She kept glancing from him to her drawing pad while he looked straight ahead at the few ladies who had gathered to gossip. One lady let out a shrill laugh and the other nodded emphatically. Good heavens but few things were as boring as watching ladies who had nothing better to do than talk about other people.

He shifted uncomfortably on the bench. "How much longer will it be until you're done?"

"Not long," Catherine assured him and reached out to nudge his chin slightly toward her. "I want to make sure I do this right."

"Is there a wrong way to draw someone?"

"No, not really, but I could make a mistake and have to start all over again."

He grimaced. He was growing restless as it was. He didn't think he had it in him to sit still for another forty minutes. "Why would you have to start over?"

"Because I want to make sure I do a good job. You're a handsome gentleman, a real pleasure to draw. I want to make sure I get everything right."

He smiled. "You think I'm handsome?"

"You have the kind of face that should be drawn."

Detecting the humor in her voice, he frowned. "Are you humoring me?"

"Of course not. I really do like the way you look. That's why I asked to draw you. When you're not around, I'll still be able to see you." After a moment of silence, she added, "I just think it's amusing you seem surprised that I think you're attractive."

"I didn't think ladies concerned themselves with how gentlemen look."

"Oh? And what did you think ladies concerned themselves with?"

He shrugged. "A gentleman's money, title, reputation…"

"Yes, those are important, but it certainly helps if a lady can glance at her husband and admire his beauty."

He rather liked that sentiment. Directing his gaze toward her, he whispered, "I admire your beauty, too."

Her face turned a most becoming shade of pink and her lips curled up into a pleased smile. Lowering her eyes, she resumed her drawing.

Taking that as his cue, he looked back to the ladies who finally decided they'd had enough of gossiping and bid each other farewell before going their separate ways.

A few minutes passed then Catherine showed him her drawing. "I'm done."

His eyes grew wide when he saw himself through her eyes. He was certain she had embellished a bit on his good points to make up for the flaws. In her drawing, his complexion was smoother, his hair perfectly in place, and his jaw a bit stronger. "This is how you see me?"

"I drew what I saw."

It was very sweet of her, and it was flattering to know that when she looked at him, this was what she saw.

"I suppose we've been here long enough," she said as she rose from the bench.

Closing the drawing pad, he handed it to her. "We could take a walk before returning home if you like."

"That'd be nice."

He offered her his arm, and she accepted it. They proceeded to enjoy a brief stroll, most of it spent in a comfortable silence, before they went home.

As they entered their townhouse, the butler handed Ethan a message. The message was addressed from Mr. Horlock, Agatha's alias.

Catherine glanced at the letter. "Mr. Horlock? Where have I heard that name before?"

He quickly tucked the letter into his pocket. "You met him briefly at Hyde Park that day when you drew those flowers."

"Oh! Yes, I remember him. He was such an odd gentleman."

"Because he's extremely shy." Motioning to the drawing pad she held, he added, "You did a wonderful job of drawing my profile."

She glanced at her pad and blushed in a way that amused him. She was simply adorable when she blushed. Turning her gaze back to him, she said, "I like drawing you."

"Well, you flattered my mother by drawing her."

"That's because I made her look a little younger, as she requested, though she's a fine looking lady regardless of her age."

"Compliments like that will get you anything you want," a lady said.

Ethan and Catherine turned around in time to see his mother walking down the hallway in their direction. Ethan crossed his arms. "Ah, Mother. You surely make it a habit of popping up when I least expect it. I thought you were visiting a friend."

"I'm done with the visit," she replied and gave Catherine a hug. "But I received a request from your father. He wants to see you, and I thought it'd do well to invite him."

Ethan grimaced. "He comes by every day."

"Not every day."

"It feels like it."

Catherine shook her head and grinned. "When will you get over your fear of him?"

"Probably never." Ethan kissed her cheek. "I think I'll see what Mr. Horlock wants."

As he headed toward the library, his mother called out, "Will you always run away when the Duke of Rumsey comes by?"

Glancing over his shoulder, he said, "It's kept me out of harm's way."

After he made it to the library, he shut the door and took Agatha's letter out of his pocket. He opened it and read it. She wanted him to go to her townhouse so she could ask him some questions to help her with the book she was currently writing. Since he owed her for all the times she'd submitted scandalous news items to the *Tittletattle* for him and because he'd much rather talk to her than take the chance of running into his father-in-law, he grabbed his cloak and left the townhouse. His mother and Catherine were chatting as they drank tea in the drawing room and probably assumed he was going to White's.

He waited until he was a couple blocks from Agatha's before he slipped the cloak around his shoulders and pulled up the hood. Keeping his head low, he took an alley. Another detour and he was at the back of her townhouse. He slipped into the servants' stairway and waited until the halls were clear before he went to her library.

She gasped as he shut the door and released her breath when he lowered the hood so she could see his face. With a laugh, she said, "I'll never get used to the way you sneak around."

He locked the door and went over to the decanter. When he saw it was empty, he shook his head. "Why isn't this full?"

Leaning back in her chair, she set her quill down on the table. "Besides you, I have no gentlemen stopping by."

"Not even a male relative?"

"Only my sister and aunt are in London this time of year."

"Oh, right. The Season. This is your sister's first Season, isn't it?"

"Yes, and she's been to many balls, though she missed the one where you got engaged."

Noting the smirk on her face, he resigned himself to doing without any wine and removed his cloak. He draped it over the back of his chair before sitting down. "You delight in the way my mother managed to get me married off, don't you?"

She shrugged and fingered her quill. "You have to admit, it has some humor in it."

"I'm glad someone thinks so." Though he still didn't think what his mother did was funny, he came to understand most people did. Clearing his throat, he motioned to the papers in front of her. "Is this the story you need help with?"

Turning serious, she straightened in her chair and sorted through the papers. As she pulled a couple out from her pile, she nodded. "I didn't expect you to come right away."

"Well, my father-in-law was on his way over to my place."

"Ah, say no more. I understand. I suppose it's my fortune that you could stop by right away."

He grabbed a glass from her tray and poured some water into it. "You need help understanding a gentleman's perspective?"

"Yes. If you suspected the lady you loved was a murderer, would you confront her?"

"Probably not. What if she lied and said no?"

"But what if she told the truth and said yes?"

"And if she was capable of murder, wouldn't she be capable of lying?"

She grinned. "Of course, but wouldn't a hero's need to protect his lady make him want to believe her?"

He leaned forward in interest. "Is your heroine a murderer?"

"No. She's innocent. It's just that her uncle made it look as if she is."

"If you want to make the book suspenseful, then the hero is going to have to wonder if she did it."

"I realize that, but I wondered if a gentleman's urge to believe in a lady's innocence would interfere with that."

"Not if he thinks she made a fool of him. If there's one thing gentlemen don't like, it's being made a fool of. We have our pride."

She shuffled another pile of papers and flipped through them. "I hadn't thought of that." She made a note on one of the papers and slipped it back into the pile. "The story would take an interesting turn if the hero suspected the heroine was making a fool of him." Looking up at him, she smiled. "This is why I like talking to you. You don't judge me for what I write, and better yet, you help me when I struggle with what I should do with the story."

"It's the least I can do for all your lies to the *Tittletattle*."

"It's a shame all those scandals didn't do you any good."

"Even so, I like to think it was worth it." He liked to think it saved him for Catherine. Turning his attention back to Agatha, he asked, "Is there anything else I can help you with?"

She scanned the papers and shook her head. "I think I have everything else I need. I should have this story ready in a month. Will you be able to take it to the publisher for me?"

"I'll be happy to." He stood up and took his cloak from the chair. "I must admit that I'm impressed you keep writing even though you haven't had a story accepted for publication yet. I know some gentlemen who would have given up already."

"When you really want something, you don't give up," she replied, smiling at him. "My family would be humiliated if they knew my secret pleasure, but it is something that brings me great joy and I see no reason to stop."

"There is no reason to stop. You have the time, talent and means. One of these days, you'll be published."

"Thank you, Ethan. You're a good friend."

He slipped into his cloak and pulled the hood up. With a nod, he unlocked the door. He made sure the hallway was clear before he snuck to the servants' stairs.

When he was safely away from Agatha's townhouse, he took off the cloak and wiped the sweat from his forehead. He draped the cloak over his arm and turned in time to see Catherine's father approaching him. His first inclination was to pretend he didn't see him and hurry to White's, but that was silly. The duke saw him look in his direction. He had to be polite enough to offer a greeting.

"Good afternoon, Your Grace," Ethan said, forcing a smile on his face.

The duke's gaze went to the cloak. "It's a little hot to be wearing a cloak, isn't it?"

He laughed. "I'm not wearing it. I'm carrying it."

"Do you take me for a fool? You have a thread from the cloak on your shoulder. That means you were wearing it."

Ethan resisted the urge to grimace. Leave it to his father-in-law to pay unnecessary attention to detail. "I caught a chill earlier, but I'm fine now."

"A chill? When it feels like mid-summer?"

"I can't explain it. My body goes from hot to cold regardless of the temperature."

The duke narrowed his eyes at him. "Really?"

"Yes. The doctor told me what my condition was, but the name is too long to pronounce." All right. Now he was so nervous that he was rattling off the stupidest lie he could think of. This had to stop. Clearing his throat, Ethan shrugged. "Well, I believe I'll be off."

"Oh? Where are you going?"

"Did you already see Catherine?"

"Yes."

"Then I'm going home."

The duke's frown deepened. "How convenient."

Ethan wasn't sure what the duke was getting at, but he decided to pretend he didn't notice the way the gentleman was scowling at him. "I hope you enjoy the rest of your day."

Though the duke didn't reply, Ethan bowed and smiled, trying his best to appear nonchalant. He turned from the duke and strode down the street, reminding himself that if he walked too fast, he'd arouse the duke's suspicions even more. Good gracious! Just what did the duke think he was doing anyway? On second thought, he didn't want to know. If his mother and Catherine didn't enjoy seeing their friends so much, he would haul them off to his country estate right away.

Oh well. September wasn't too far off. He only had to bear with the duke until then. He wiped the sweat from his forehead again, this time uncertain if it was because he was hot or because he was dreading seeing the duke again.

Chapter Eighteen

*I*n June, Catherine woke up, entangled in Ethan's bed sheets and wrapped in his arms. Had it been cooler in the room, such a situation would have been welcoming. But since it was warm, she was sweaty, and being sweaty led to quite a degree of discomfort. She pushed a sleeping Ethan away from her and fought the sheets until she was free. Sitting up in the bed, she fanned her face and scanned the dark room until her gaze settled on the closed window. Well, there was the problem. The wind had blown the window shut.

Collecting a few pins from the small table by the bed, she pulled her hair back and pinned it to the top of her head. The absence of hair on her neck and back was an immediate relief, but she needed fresh air. She slipped off the bed and went to the window. She opened it, making sure it locked into place so the wind wouldn't close it again. The cool wind felt like heaven against her skin, so she stood in front of the window.

"Get away from there!"

Surprised, she turned and saw Ethan gesturing for her to get away from the window. "I don't need anyone seeing my naked wife."

"Oh." She hadn't thought someone might see her. She peered out the window. "There's no one out there. I think everyone's asleep."

He groaned and sat up. "Will you please come back to bed?"

She stepped away from the window but let the cool air wafting into the room cool her back. "I can't sleep when I'm sweaty. I need to cool off first."

"You'll be the death of me yet."

"Why? No one can see me from here."

Through the moonlight, she saw his exasperated expression. "And people think I have no sense of propriety. Catherine, I forbid you to go anywhere near the window when you're not fully clothed, unless the curtains are drawn."

Pleased, she walked over to the bed and climbed in. "What if you happened to be the person out there?" She straddled him, making sure his erection was nestled between her legs, and wrapped her arms around his neck. "Would you want me to linger over there?"

"That's irrelevant."

"Is it?"

She moved her hips, her sensitive nub rubbing his shaft. When he moaned in pleasure, she leaned forward and kissed him. His flesh was warm, and even though the room was still stuffy, she didn't mind. When she was making love to him, she didn't mind the heat so much. It was when she slept that she preferred to be cool.

When the kiss ended, he wrapped his arms around her so her breasts pressed against his chest. "If I am the only one at the window, then I'll be very happy to watch you dance around in all your naked glory."

Her lips curled up. "Dance around? I wasn't dancing around just now?"

"You might as well have been with the way your breasts were jiggling."

"Do you like my breasts?" She wondered if he found them lacking since they weren't as big as what most ladies had but had been too timid to ask the question before. Now, it seemed like a good time.

"Of course, I do." He brought one of his hands to her breast and cupped it in his hand. "What's not to like? It's soft." He brushed his thumb against her nipple, sending a shiver of delight straight to her core. "And sensitive." With a wicked grin, he added, "I love your breasts."

He bowed his head and brought his mouth to her nipple. He kissed it before he traced his tongue over it and gently tugged on it with his teeth. She gasped and squirmed against him, aware of his strengthening erection. She rocked her hips until her nub was firmly over him and focused on the way he tweaked and tugged at her nipple. His hand went to her other nipple, his fingers gently squeezing it, making the ache between her legs unbearable.

"Ethan," she whispered.

He wrapped his arms around her and rolled her onto her back. Leaning over her, he continued his ministrations over one of her nipples while bringing his hand between her legs. He found her sensitive nub and caressed it. Two fingers slid into her core, and he stroked her. She grasped his arms, threw her head back and moaned. Her climax came quickly, crashing into her, engulfing her in a heightened state of pleasure. She loved how he could make her feel weak and powerful all at once. And he continued to stroke her core and suck on her nipple to prolong the sensations pulsating through her body.

When she'd ridden the last wave of pleasure, he shifted so that he was between her legs and entered her, slow and purposeful until he was fully inside her. Her flesh tightened around him and she lifted her hips to better feel him. He clasped her hands over her head and moved his hips, continuing to take it slow. She became aware of the tension mounting inside her as he stroked her, the ridge at the bottom of his tip working against the sensitive area in her core. Her hips rose to meet him, aiding him along as he established a rhythm, going in and out, building to a faster pace.

In time, his movements grew faster, his thrusting more insistent, silently demanding she climax again. And she did. She cried out and her core squeezed him, her body shuddering beneath him. He gave her one last thrust before he let out his own cry and stiffened, releasing his seed into her. She opened her eyes and watched him. He was utterly handsome when he was receiving pleasure from her body.

When he collapsed in her arms, she smiled and pressed her cheek to his. Yes, she was sweaty. More so than before, but she certainly didn't mind it. Tomorrow, they'd bathe, preferably together, and she would cool off then. He remained inside her, something she loved since it made her feel intimately connected to him, and before long, he fell asleep. Though she was still awake, she smiled and continued to hold him. She loved him. She didn't know when it happened. They'd spent a considerable amount of time together since getting married. Somewhere along the way, she'd given him her heart. She could only hope that in due time, he might give her his as well.

***

A week later while Catherine was visiting Lady Roderick, Ethan decided to read a book. He chose a couch to lounge in and got comfortable. He was in the middle of reading "The Rime of the Ancient Mariner" in *Lyrical Ballads, With a Few Other Poems* when the door to his library flew open.

"Ethan!"

Startled, he released the book which soared across the room and landed somewhere near the fireplace. He couldn't tell exactly where it landed because his heart was racing too fast and his vision blurred as someone grabbed his arms and shook him.

"Lady Hettinwood is going to have a grandchild!"

It took him a full thirty seconds to realize it was his mother who was shaking him and using a shrill voice that would wake the dead. Pulling her away, he straightened on the couch in an effort to regain his composure.

"Mother, settle yourself down."

Who would have thought a grown gentleman could be scared witless because his mother burst into his library in the middle of the day? He helped her into the chair across from him then settled back onto the couch, feeling much better.

"All right. You have my full attention," he began. "What is this about Lady Hettinwood?"

"She's going to have a grandchild! And her son only married last month." She pointed her finger at him. "That's one month less than you've been married."

Unable to believe this was the cause for concern, he stared at her for a long moment.

"Don't you understand?" his mother insisted, wringing her hands. "You have been married longer than her son, and you don't have a grandchild on the way."

"Oh, Mother!" He shook his head, not believing his ears. "This has nothing to do with an heir. It's about your ongoing feud with your friend." He paused before adding, "I wouldn't even call her a friend."

"She is a friend."

"Well, you two have the oddest friendship I've ever seen. You're in competition with each other, and yet, you can't seem to live without her."

"I've known her for years. We knew each other before our first Season."

He held up his hand to stop her from saying anything else. "I'm aware of the four-decade rivalry you two share. What I don't understand is why you visit her."

"Never mind about my friendship with her," she replied. "I'm here to talk about you. When are you going to give me a grandchild?"

"I can't predict when Catherine will get with child." Really, like he could control such a thing!

"But are you doing your part?"

"Of course, I am!"

"Then why isn't she expecting a child yet?"

With a groan, he gave her a pointed look. "This is absurd. I can't do anything more than what I am doing to give you a grandchild. And really, Mother. You ought to be ashamed of yourself. Wanting a grandchild so you can compete with your friend!"

"Don't turn this on me. I have a legitimate concern. Most ladies conceive right after the wedding ceremony. I just want to be sure you're doing everything you can to make it happen with Catherine."

"There have been a couple ladies who didn't conceive at all. Not everyone has children."

"But are you making the effort, Ethan?" she pressed, a determined look in her eye insisting he assure her that he was.

Despite the heat rising up to his face, he said, "Yes."

"But you have to make the effort more than once a month."

"Mother, I assure you that I am doing everything I can. No one can make a greater effort than I am."

"Then why isn't Catherine expecting yet?"

"We've only been married for two months!" Honestly, the lady could beat a point to death!

"But Lady Hettinwood's son has only been married for a month."

Deciding he'd had enough of his mother's nagging, he stood up. "I have said all I care to say regarding this matter.

Now, if you'll please leave me to my reading, I'll be ever so grateful."

She grunted, a dissatisfied expression on her face, and rose to her feet. "You aren't having any…issues…getting things done in bed, are you?"

His jaw dropped. "What?"

"Because if you are, I know of a doctor who might be able to help you…you know…finish the job."

He gasped. She couldn't be implying he might be impotent! Oh, of course she was! "I forbid you from thinking such a horrible thought. Do you hear me? Get that thought right out of your mind this instant."

Her face fell. "Then it's true."

By now he was ready to pull his hair out. He stormed over to her, hands clenched at his sides, steam coming out of his ears. "No, it's not! Why don't you ever listen to me? I tell you what's going on, but you don't listen. I might as well be talking to the wind."

"Can you ensure that Catherine is expecting by the end of this month?"

He threw his hands up in the air. The wind. She was just like the wind! He couldn't reason with her any more than he could reason with the wind. It did what it wanted, blowing hot or cold, fiercely or softly. There was no rhyme or reason to it. It simply did its thing, much like she did hers. And once it was determined to blow in a certain direction, it didn't stop until it was done. Why did he even try? He'd be better off locking his door so she could never enter the library. Yes, that's what he'd do! He'd start locking his door and stuff his ears with something so he wouldn't have to listen to her bang on his door.

Turning his attention to the door, he realized that it'd been open the whole time his mother had been pestering him. He motioned to the door and hissed, "Are you satisfied? That door has been open the whole time. Now the whole house knows what we've been saying."

A scandal of a different sort might stem from this if the servants talked. Maybe he could give them extra money in exchange for their silence. The irony wasn't lost to him. He used to slip stories here and there and pray the servants would spread rumors of his indiscretions around London. And now he was trying to think of ways to get them to keep quiet.

At that moment, he heard the door in the entryway open. Was the butler running off to spread the gossip already? He moaned and rubbed his eyes. Why couldn't he be out in the country where life was simple and quiet? At least out there, the servants had no one to talk to but themselves.

"Good afternoon, my lady," the butler said.

Catherine returned the greeting.

Ethan turned back to his mother. "I don't want you bothering Catherine about this grandchild nonsense. Is that understood?"

His mother's eyes widened. "Why? Will she tell me you haven't been diligent about giving me one?" she whispered.

"No," he hissed. "But it's embarrassing you'd even ask. It's one thing for you to harass me this way, but I won't have you doing it to her."

She opened her mouth to speak, but Catherine showed up in the doorway of the library. "I have something wonderful to tell you," Catherine said, her face glowing with excitement as she entered the room and went over to Ethan. "I didn't want to say anything sooner in case I was wrong, but now I've confirmed it and can safely tell you. I'm with child! Isn't that wonderful?"

Ethan nearly collapsed with relief. Good. He was spared his mother's nagging and the servants from gossiping. "That is wonderful, my dear." He kissed her and looked at his mother. "Isn't that wonderful, Mother?"

His mother embraced Catherine and patted her back. "Catherine, I'm so delighted to hear this!" When she pulled away from her, she clasped her hands and added, "It's so nice to know you managed to get the job done."

Catherine's eyebrows furrowed and she glanced at Ethan, a silent question in her eyes about what his mother meant.

Ethan waved the question aside. "Mother was in hysterics because Lord Hettinwood's son's wife is with child. But thanks to you, she can relax."

"Oh. All right," Catherine hesitantly replied.

"It doesn't matter," he assured her. "How was your day with Lady Roderick?"

"Good. She and her husband are having a ball in two weeks. Can we go?"

"Of course, we can." Even if going to balls still wasn't among his favorite things to do, he knew it would mean a lot to Catherine that she got to go.

"Only if you feel up to it," his mother added, patting Catherine's hand. "You don't want to do too much now that you're in the family way."

"I feel fine," Catherine replied. "And I really want to go." She turned back to Ethan. "This will be the first ball I'll go to where I won't have to feel awkward. I'll have someone to talk to and dance with. For the first time in my life, I can look forward to it."

He grinned, pleased by the way her cheeks grew pink and eyes twinkled. "We'll have a good time," he told her, noting that her smile grew wider.

"Well, I think I'll pay one of my friends a visit," his mother said after she gave Catherine another hug. Cupping Catherine's face in her hands, she kissed her cheek. "You, my dear, are a godsend."

As his mother left, Catherine directed her gaze to him. "What was all that about?"

"No one can know for sure when it comes to my mother," he lied. Like he'd tell Catherine about his mother's need to compete with Lady Hettinwood! "At least she's happy."

"Yes, that's true."

He went to the fireplace and retrieved the book he'd been reading when his mother so rudely interrupted him.

"What are you reading?" Catherine asked, approaching him.

"Just some poems." He showed the book to her. "My mother assumes I read literature unfitting for a lady, so you must never tell her I read something she'd approve of."

"Why, that's silly." She giggled and squeezed his arm affectionately. "However, I promised to honor my word about your reputation. Your secret is safe with me."

He kissed her and returned the book to its rightful place on the bookshelf. "What would you like to do today?"

"Would you mind taking me to the circus again? There's a show in one hour."

His eyebrows rose in surprise. "You enjoyed it that much?"

"I did. Will you take me?"

He took in her hopeful expression, her eyes lit with anticipation, her lips curled up, her hands clasped together over her chest. How could he deny such an angel anything? "Of course, I'll take you."

"Thank you!" She kissed him and hurried for the door. "I won't take long to change!"

Chuckling, he watched her, pleased he could make her happy.

Chapter Nineteen

$\mathcal{N}$ext to Ethan, Catherine squealed in delight as the acrobats performed their stunts. He grinned, more from her reaction than from the impressive feats the acrobats employed on the tightrope and swings. Catherine had no idea how adorable she was, and he still couldn't get over how different she was from the lady he had danced with every Season. If he had any idea she wasn't as boring as she pretended to be, he would have sought her hand during her first Season. Oh well. Nothing could be done about the past. The important thing was that he was with her now, and better yet, she was expecting a child. In one fell swoop, she managed to appease his mother, save his reputation with the servants, and possibly give him an heir.

He glanced her way and their eyes met. Leaning forward, he whispered in her ear, "It's a shame I never took the time to get to know you better sooner."

He noted the way she prettily blushed and his smile widened. Turning his attention back to the center of the circus, he saw the acrobats finish their routine. Afterwards, a man named Iron Jim ran into the center of the ring to announce the next performance.

"Ladies and gentlemen, have we got a treat for you," Iron Jim's voice boomed. "I present to you the best juggler in the entire world. I make no idle boast. But why believe me? You'll have to see it for yourself. I introduce Willie, the juggler who can juggle anything!"

The crowd cheered as Willie, who had graying hair and a bounce to his step, came into the center of the ring. Four clowns followed him, two trying to carry a table but kept tripping or dropping the table in an effort to make the audience laugh. Their tactic worked well, for Catherine giggled in amusement. Ethan had to admit that the show was better the second time around, even if he knew what to expect.

Two other clowns stumbled and almost dropped the bowls of items they were carrying. While two clowns finally managed to set the table, the ones carrying the bowls made a show of attempting a trade that neither seemed happy with. Finally, the clowns who set the table chased the ones carrying the bowls until they set the items Willie would juggle on the table.

"I don't know which I enjoy more," Catherine told Ethan as she chuckled. "Watching those clowns or the juggler."

"Everything they do, it's to keep you entertained, so you might as well enjoy all of it," he replied over the audience's laughter.

The clowns bowed and cleared the stage so Willie could become the focus of the act. The drum rolled as he picked up the balls. He made a show of juggling the balls, adding more from time to time. Afterwards, he juggled some fruit and made a show of turning around and tossing them under his legs.

When he was done, Iron Jim jogged over to him. Turning to the audience, he said, "Balls and fruits are mildly amusing, Willie. Surely, we can do better than that."

"Balls and fruits are what you gave me," Willie retorted with a huff. "If you can't come up with a good idea, then maybe someone in the audience can."

"A challenge for the fine people in our audience today?" Iron Jim's smile widened as he turned back to the crowd. "Don't be shy, folks. Willie's questioning my integrity. I promised you that he could juggle anything, and I meant it. But it seems that he needs something a bit more difficult."

"A lot more difficult, please. I'm getting bored up here," Willie added, making the audience laugh again.

"There you have it," Iron Jim said. "Give Willie something difficult so he'll shut up and leave me alone."

From the audience, Ethan heard someone call out, "Knives!"

Ethan looked in the direction from where the gentleman spoke and realized it was Christopher. A smile tugged at his lips. Leave it to Christopher to suggest something dangerous.

Iron Jim clapped his hands together. "Ah, a very wise choice. What is your name, sir?"

"Mr. Robinson," Christopher called out.

"Very good, Mr. Robinson." Iron Jim turned to one of the clowns. "Bring out the knives!"

The audience grew silent and watched as a clown brought the knives out. Catherine grasped Ethan's arm and whispered, "I don't recall knives from before."

"That's because no one suggested them last time," Ethan replied. "This part of the performance is based on what the audience wants."

"But aren't knives too dangerous?"

He shook his head. "Not for Willie. He's experienced at this."

"And just so no one thinks the knives are fake," Iron Jim began, directing Ethan's attention back to him, "I'll cut my very own hat." He proceeded to do as promised.

A drum roll accompanied Willie as he lifted the four knives and juggled them. Catherine's fingers dug into Ethan's arm, but he hardly noticed since he couldn't take his eyes off of Willie who expertly tossed and caught the knives as if he was handling the balls.

When Willie was done, Catherine and Ethan

enthusiastically clapped with everyone else.

Iron Jim held up his hand to silence everyone. "Maybe someone can come up with something a little more challenging. Knives, after all, are too easy, aren't they, Willie?"

"They are, but I love how well they cut fruit," Willie replied.

Willie then picked up two knives and two apples, and while juggling, he cut one apple and ate slices of it, not missing a beat the entire time. When he was done eating both apples, he set the knives down and bowed for the cheering crowd.

"But that's too simple. You need something harder than that," Iron Jim said with a hearty laugh. "Now, who can come up with something harder?"

Catherine tugged on Ethan's arm. "Can he juggle fire?"

Ethan nodded and called out, "Fire!"

Iron Jim clapped his hands together and rubbed them. "Ah, a gentleman who lives a little more dangerously. What is your name, sir?"

"Lord Edon."

"Bring out the fire," Iron Jim called out to the clowns. "I bet Lord Edon doesn't believe Willie can do it, but we don't call Willie 'the juggler who can juggle anything' for no reason. We assure you, my lord, that we don't make the boast in vain."

The clowns lit three torches and brought them to Willie. Catherine's grip tightened once more on Ethan's arm. Willie took the torches one by one and tossed them in the air, quickly establishing a rhythm.

"Are you challenged yet?" Iron Jim asked him.

Willie shook his head. "It's too simple!"

The crowd laughed and cheered while Iron Jim called for another torch. Soon Willie had added another.

"How can he do that?" Catherine whispered in awe.

"Because he truly is the best," Ethan replied. "Apparently, Iron Jim didn't make an idle boast after all."

"I should say not! He's magnificent!"

"He is."

"I'm glad you took me."

"I'd take you anywhere if it means you'll be happy."

She gave him a smile that melted his heart. He returned her smile and held her hand. She leaned against him, and they continued to enjoy the rest of the show.

***

The next day Catherine decided to visit her father. As much as she wanted to bring Ethan with her, she knew neither her father nor Ethan would like that, so she went alone. When the footman opened the door of her carriage, she got out and hurried up the steps to his townhouse. To her surprise, her father opened the door and embraced her.

"Have you decided to flee from your husband? You know you can always stay here," he said as he released her.

She giggled. "Oh Father, that's not necessary. I'm very happy with Ethan."

He grimaced at the mention of her husband's name. "You don't need to be brave. You can tell me the truth."

As she walked into the entryway, she greeted the footman and butler. Turning to her father who followed her into his townhouse, she said, "I am telling you the truth. Why is it so hard for you to believe me?"

Her father looked at the butler. "We'll have some tea and scones in the drawing room."

The butler bowed and headed for the kitchen.

"Come. We'll talk in private," her father said as he took her arm and gently led her to the drawing room. Once there, he shut the door and turned to her. "Now, you may tell me the truth. Do you seek refuge?"

She groaned and sat on the settee, placing her reticule beside her. "No. I am not leaving my husband."

"But you can. At any time…for any reason. I'll understand."

"Why is it so hard for you to believe I'm happy with him?"

He sat in the chair across from her, his shoulders slumped. "If your husband was an honorable gentleman, I wouldn't fret so."

"You're a wonderful father, truly you are. You never held it against me that I wasn't a son, and you did all you could to secure a good husband for me. I appreciate all you've done."

His eyebrows furrowed. "I don't know if I like the sound of this or not."

She shifted so that she was more comfortable. "I only meant to convey my gratitude for how much you love me. And I want to reassure you that Ethan takes very good care of me, much like the way you always have."

He pressed his hand to his stomach. "I never thought I'd be compared to the likes of him."

It was unfortunate she couldn't tell him the truth about Ethan, that he wasn't the scoundrel her father thought he was, but she'd given her word to Ethan and she'd rather die than break it.

There was a knock at the door, and her father told the person to enter. The butler came into the room and placed the scones and tea on the table between her and her father. After he poured the tea into their cups, he handed her a cup and smiled. "You look like you're doing well, my lady," he said.

"I am, thank you." She blew the tea to cool it before she took a sip. "It's as delicious as I remember."

Her father accepted his cup. "Thank you," he told the butler. "That will be all."

The butler bowed and left, closing the door behind him.

Her father let out a heavy sigh and placed the cup back on the tray. "Catherine, it's been difficult for me to leave you in that townhouse. Many times, I wanted to go over there and bring you back to safety. Tell me, is that…gentleman…you married discrete when he goes out to do his business?"

She took another sip of her tea before holding the cup in her lap. "Why don't you listen to me? You fret over nothing. I keep telling you that I'm happy, and I came over here to tell you good news."

"Good news? You and your husband have decided to live in separate residences?"

Surprised that should be considered good news to him, she laughed. "Goodness, Father, no. That wouldn't be good news."

"It would be for me."

"Father, I came to tell you that I'm expecting a child!"

He winced and then he relaxed. "Yes, I can see why you'd consider that good news. Now he can leave you alone."

It took her a moment to understand that he'd imagined many horrors had befallen her in the bedchamber with Ethan and that since she was with child, Ethan could finally stop coming to her bed. She'd heard that some ladies dreaded the bed but felt the need to do their duty to the crown, so they gritted their teeth and endured lovemaking. But that was nothing like what she experienced. She wondered if she was the only lady who enjoyed being intimate with her husband.

"I'll pray you have a son," her father continued, breaking her from her thoughts. "A healthy one, of course. With any luck, you will be spared from having to go through the process of trying for another child." After a moment, he added in a hesitant tone, "Was your husband gentle with you?"

She knew very well she couldn't come out and tell him that she anticipated her moments alone with Ethan. For one, he'd never believe it. And two, it didn't seem appropriate to discuss such personal matters with her father. As it was, he couldn't bring himself to accept the fact that she was happy with Ethan. Finally, she decided to simply state the truth, hoping he accepted it. "Yes, Father, he was gentle with me."

By the relief on his face, she was assured he did, indeed, accept it, and she was more than relieved to know he finally believed Ethan could do something good.

Eager to talk about the impending arrival of her child, she turned the conversation to the names she was considering giving the child. The ploy worked, and soon they were having a good discussion, much like the ones they had enjoyed in the past.

After she left his townhouse, she was debating whether or not to leave a request to visit Claire when she saw Claire leaving her townhouse. She tapped on the ceiling of the carriage to signal the driver to stop. As her carriage stopped, she waved to Claire from her window. Claire headed in her direction, and Catherine's footman opened the carriage door in time for her to call out a greeting.

"Good afternoon, Lady Roderick! I was hoping to have a word with you. Do you have time or should we talk later?"

"I was on my way shopping and wouldn't mind the company," Claire replied.

"I can take you since I'm out anyway."

"Let me tell my footman to put my carriage back."

Catherine nodded and sat back in her seat as she waited for her friend to return. When she did, Catherine asked, "Where do you want to shop?"

"Rundell, Bridge and Rundell. I'm getting my husband a new pocket watch."

"Tell the driver to take us to Rundell, Bridge, and Rundell," Catherine told the footman.

He indicated he would and shut the door, finally giving Catherine time alone with Claire. She waited until the coachman urged the horses forward before speaking.

"Claire, we've only known each other for a short time, but I was wondering if I might ask you something of a personal nature?"

Claire set her reticule on the seat and clasped her hands in her lap. Interested, she turned her full attention to Catherine. "Of course. What is it?"

"Well…" She'd never actively discussed anything like this with someone. Sure, her mother-in-law was open about what happened in the bedchamber on the day she married Ethan, but after that, her mother-in-law hadn't said anything else on topic. And Catherine wasn't about to confide in her. It seemed inappropriate to talk to a mother about her son in that way. So really, her only option was to talk to Claire, and if Claire decided the topic was too personal, Catherine would forget the matter. Gathering her courage, Catherine glanced away from her friend and murmured, "Do you enjoy being intimate with your husband?"

"Do I enjoy what?" Claire pressed, leaning forward. "I'm sorry, Catherine, but I didn't hear everything you said."

Forcing her voice to be louder, she asked her question again, her face warming as she did so.

"Yes, I do," Claire replied.

Relieved, Catherine finally made eye contact with her friend. "You do?"

"I just said I did. What is this about?"

"You'll think it's silly, but I thought I was the only lady who enjoyed the marital bed. I thought maybe there was something wrong with me."

"I can see why you thought that. It's not something we're encouraged to discuss. Well, my sister doesn't mind discussing it, but then she's always been outspoken when it's just the two of us. But rest assured that you're not the only lady who enjoys moments alone with her husband."

The tension in Catherine's body eased, and she smiled. "I'm glad I can talk freely with you."

Claire returned her smile. "If you can't talk to your friends, who can you talk to?" After a moment, she asked, "Are you happy with your husband…outside the bedchamber?"

"I am. My father doesn't believe me, no matter how often I tell him. He might never accept my marriage. Ethan is completely different from what I thought he was. I'm not at liberty to say how. I made a promise to him I wouldn't, but I was very pleased when I discovered his true nature."

"I'm glad to hear it. I think we enjoy intimate moments with our husbands because we enjoy our time with them outside the bedchamber."

The carriage came to a stop, and Catherine looked out the window. "We're here. Maybe I should give Ethan a gift, too. His birthday is coming up soon."

"I don't see any reason why you shouldn't. There's no reason why ladies should receive all the gifts."

Deciding she'd also get Ethan a pocket watch, she waited for the footman to open the door and left the carriage with Claire to do some shopping.

Chapter Twenty

*E*than hurried to the Western Exchange. It was already a couple minutes past two. If his mother hadn't delayed him with talk of naming the baby, he would have been here sooner. Sneaking out to help Agatha was proving to be harder ever since he got married. Fortunately, Catherine was busy fitting a dress for the ball that night at Lord and Lady Roderick's. He didn't know why Catherine fretted over the right dress to wear. It wasn't like she was still trying to find a husband, but she claimed that she wanted to look good for him. It was sweet she thought of him, so he didn't mind. And truth be told, it worked to his advantage since he only had to deal with his mother on the way out of the townhouse. Too bad his mother didn't agonize over what dress to wear when she went to balls.

Ethan pushed the thought aside as he arrived at the Western Exchange where merchants sold their wares at different booths. Ignoring them, he scanned the crowd for Agatha who said she'd be dressed as Mr. Horlock. He found her in her disguise soon enough, and to his surprise, she was talking to Christopher. Ethan headed in their direction. Christopher, the first one to look in his direction, waved a greeting to him.

"You're unusually happy," Agatha said, using her Mr. Horlock voice.

"It's a pleasant day," Ethan replied with a shrug. "The sun's out, people are smiling, colors are more vibrant—"

Christopher laughed. "Colors are more vibrant?"

"They are," Ethan insisted.

"I think your wife has something to do with that ridiculous grin on your face," Christopher said with a snicker.

Ethan sighed. He should have known his friend couldn't refuse the opportunity to tease him.

"And to think that two months ago, you were bemoaning the fact that you had to go to the church to read the Banns," Christopher continued.

"He was bemoaning it?" Agatha asked.

Like she didn't know! But since she was supposed to be Mr. Horlock, she had to play the part of the gentleman who didn't know any of this.

"His bride was crying, her father was glowering at him, and he kept wincing as if he were in pain," Christopher told her.

Just as Ethan suspected, Christopher had enjoyed the whole sordid affair. He thought he saw amusement on Christopher's face that day.

She joined Christopher in laughing. "That must have been a sight! I'm sorry I missed it."

Deciding not to let Christopher bother him, he gave an exaggerated shrug. "There might have been a little uncertainty going into the marriage."

"Your bride sobbed through the whole thing," Christopher added, which made her laugh harder than before.

"Tears of joy...at least as time went on," Ethan replied. Eager to put the matter to rest, he turned to Agatha. "However, I'm not here to discuss my marriage. I hear you have a manuscript for me."

She grew serious and cleared her throat. "Yes. I appreciate your taking the time to do this."

"Do what?" Christopher asked as she handed the manuscript to Ethan.

Ethan decided to answer for her. "I know the publisher of Minerva Press and told him I knew a talented author whose manuscript I'd deliver to him."

"Just because he knows the publisher, it doesn't mean he'll accept my manuscript," she clarified. "He rejected the other manuscripts I wrote."

"If you don't mind my being so bold, what do you write?" Christopher asked her.

"Gothic horror with some," she lowered her voice, "romance in it."

"Some what?"

"Romance in it."

"What is that book about?"

"The usual. A castle reported to be haunted, a heroine whose life is in danger, a hero who saves her," she mumbled. "Things you wouldn't be interested in," she rushed out. "I must take my leave." She turned to Ethan and bowed. "Thank you, Lord Edon."

"What a strange gentleman," Christopher commented as she scurried away as if her rear end had caught on fire.

"Yes, Mr. Horlock is stranger than you think," Ethan replied, wondering what Christopher would do if he knew the truth. "And you needn't keep laughing over what happened at my wedding. Catherine and I are quite happy now."

"I hear that her father is still distraught."

"There's nothing I can do about him."

"I suppose not, but at least he isn't making you clean stables or chamber pots."

"You're never going to forgive Lord Roderick for doing that, are you?" Ethan asked as they strolled by some of the booths.

"I like to think 'forget' is a better word," Christopher replied. "Forgiveness is something I have to do. Every Sunday I'm reminded to do that, but I think I can remember what happened since I never want to fall under Lord Roderick's bad graces again."

"Speaking of Lord Roderick, do you plan to attend his ball tonight?"

"My guardian requires it, so I have no choice."

Surprised, Ethan stopped and studied him. "Lord Clement is making you go? Why?"

"Probably so he can keep an eye on me. He's afraid I'll get into a brawl or something worse. Just because I upset a couple of gentlemen in the past, it doesn't mean I still go around drinking and spouting my mouth off."

Resisting the urge to chuckle since he had to admit Christopher did say some of the funniest things when he had been drunk in the past, Ethan cleared his throat. With a solemn expression, he said, "It's not good to get drunk anyway. That's how most gentlemen lose their money at the gambling hells. Part of my secret to winning so many games was that I didn't drink while playing."

"I don't get drunk anymore. I know better. My guardian would have me stay at Lord Roderick's again." He went over to a booth where a merchant was selling leather gloves. "I could use new gloves when I go horse riding. How much for a pair?" he asked the merchant.

The merchant told him the price.

He groaned and put them back on the table and looked at Ethan. "My guardian doesn't allow me enough money to do anything."

"I'll buy you the gloves," Ethan said.

"You will?"

"Yes, but with the stipulation that you must never mention chamber pots or cleaning stables ever again when I'm around."

Christopher hesitated, his gaze going from the gloves to Ethan then back to the gloves. Finally, he sighed. "All right. I agree to your requirement."

"Good." Ethan paid for the gloves and gave them to his friend. "There. Now, you can ride your horse and look fashionable." As they left the booth, he caught sight of a booth with a drawing pad and pencils. "I think I'll buy Catherine a gift while I'm here."

"Things must really be going well with you and your wife if you're buying something for her. Unless you're hoping she'll go off into a corner somewhere and draw so she leaves you alone."

He grinned at the teasing tone in his friend's voice. "I would never do that to her. She's a lovely lady. I wouldn't mind it if you went off into a corner, though," he joked.

"It's a sad state of affairs when a gentleman thinks he's funny and he's not," Christopher retorted.

Ignoring him, Ethan went to the other booth and paid for a new pad and some pencils to give to Catherine.

"Thank you for the gloves," Christopher said, "and I'll see you tonight at Lord Roderick's."

Ethan nodded and made his purchase. Once he did, he went to Minerva Press to drop off Agatha's story then went to the townhouse to get ready for the ball.

***

It was the first ball Ethan and Catherine attended since their wedding, and Ethan had to admit going to a ball wasn't so bad with her by his side. Tonight no eager mothers would be trying to pair him up with their daughters since he was already married.

Catherine squeezed his arm affectionately. "Thank you for bringing me here," she said as they entered the ballroom.

Noting the excitement in her eyes, he smiled. "You're beautiful."

She glanced at her blue gown. "Claire helped me pick this out."

"No. I didn't mean the dress. I meant you. You're beautiful."

Her face grew pink, and she lowered her gaze.

He tipped her chin upward and whispered, "You're a very lovely person, both to look at and to be with."

"What a splendid ball," his mother exclaimed, coming up behind him.

He gave a slight jerk. "Mother, I wish you wouldn't creep up on me like that." It seemed to him the lady delighted in startling him.

She waved aside his comment and focused on Catherine. "Is your father planning to attend this ball?"

"I think so," she replied.

"Good. I'll go see if I can find him. I'd like to see how he's faring since he last visited."

As she left, Ethan considered asking Catherine if she wanted to dance, but Lady Roderick approached her. "I'm glad you could make it."

Catherine turned to her friend and started talking. Ethan tuned them out and scanned the room to see who else was there. He didn't want to be dragged into talking to Lord Roderick or anyone else who might bore him with a political discussion. He found a couple gentlemen who frequented the gambling hells. They cared for politics as much as he did.

He offered Catherine and Lady Roderick a smile before he went over to the three gentlemen who were laughing. When he reached them, he realized Lord Carlisle was detailing his trip to Spain.

"Oh, Lord Edon," he began when he looked in his direction, "have you had the pleasure of watching a bull fight?"

"If you're referring to my latest encounter with my father-in-law, then not only have I watched a bull fight but I've been at the mercy of a bull," Ethan joked.

The others laughed.

"And yet you remain unharmed," Lord Carlisle replied. "You're in one piece."

"So far I've managed to dodge him, yes."

"Come now," Lord Burke said with a shake of his head, "surely His Grace is grateful you married his daughter."

"You'd think so," Ethan commented, his gaze traveling the room, finding his father-in-law talking to Catherine. Good thing he got out of harm's way when he did!

"I don't envy you," Lord Carlisle said. "His Grace isn't a gentleman I'd want in my family. I'd rather take my chances with a real bull."

"You'd stand a better chance of living that way," Ethan agreed.

As Lord Carlisle responded, Ethan happened to see Agatha pass by with her sister. Since she gave him a slight nod to indicate she wanted him to introduce the gentlemen to her sister, he waved to her. "Lady Richfield, might we have a moment of your time?"

She paused, her sister following suit, and the two approached them.

After Ethan introduced the gentlemen to the ladies, he added, "Lord Carlisle loves to travel. In fact, he just returned from Spain."

"Did he?" Agatha glanced at her sister with raised eyebrows. "My sister went to Spain three years ago."

"She did?" Lord Carlisle turned his gaze to her sister and smiled. "What did you think of it?"

"It was beautiful country," her sister shyly replied.

"Perhaps we should discuss it while we dance?" he offered.

She accepted, and the two headed for the middle of the room.

Ethan glanced at Agatha. He knew she dreaded the thought of dancing with any of the remaining gentlemen because she didn't want to encourage any of them. Turning to the gentlemen, he said, "I hate to see a lady without a dance partner." He offered her his arm. "May I?"

Agatha nodded and accepted. Once they were dancing, she asked, "So you really are happy being a married gentleman?"

He grinned, his gaze going to Catherine who was laughing at something Lady Roderick told her. "I am. I didn't think I'd be, but my wife is perfect."

"It's a shame not all marriages result in love."

"I didn't think mine would."

"I know. You thought your life was about to come to an end."

He chuckled, returning his attention to her. "It was silly how I reacted, now that I think about it."

"Well, you were giving up your dream of living a quiet life in the country so you could escape the chaos that is London."

"Yes, that was my dream, but I find I don't mind London so much now that I don't have to put up a huge pretense of being a notorious rake."

"There's nothing like a wife to straighten a gentleman's path."

"Or make it so that he can straighten his path without looking as if he was a fraud to begin with." And that was a surprising discovery. He didn't think he'd care for the role of the honorable gentleman, but he found it actually suited him just fine.

"I'll consent to that," she replied.

"And what of you?" Ethan asked. "What brings you out to a ball? I thought you'd rather pull out all of your hair than be here."

"My sister was in need of a chaperone."

"Ah. You're a good sister to bring her here."

"Ethan," she began, after glancing over her shoulder, "how well do you know Mr. Robinson?"

"I wondered when you'd ask me about him since you were talking to him when you gave me your book earlier today."

"It was a meeting by chance."

"I thought as much. You wouldn't go around dressed as a gentleman so you could chat with other gentlemen."

"You seem to know him well."

"We go to White's, and we play cards from time to time. He's an affable fellow if you're looking for someone suitable for your sister, though he lacks a title."

"Maybe…"

"If you wish, I could introduce him to your sister."

"They were introduced," she replied. "She fancies Lord Dabney, so she danced with him instead of Mr. Robinson."

He noted the nonchalant way she said Mr. Robinson's name and suspected a hint of interest in her voice. "Oh, then you were inquiring about Mr. Robinson because you've taken an interest in him?"

"Of course not!"

The music ended, and he bowed. With a glance at Catherine who was still talking to Lady Roderick, he wondered if it would be wise to approach her. Before he could make a decision either way, the Duke of Rumsey hurried over to him, and by the scowl on his face, Ethan knew this wasn't going to be a pleasant encounter.

Chapter Twenty-One

"Why were you dancing with someone who isn't your wife?" Catherine's father demanded, his jaw clenched and hands clasped in front of him.

"It's a ball, Your Grace," Ethan replied, not knowing whether he should laugh or be intimidated. "Gentlemen dance with ladies, ladies they aren't married to."

"Which isn't a problem unless the gentleman in question has a reputation for being London's most notorious rake. Considering your past, I don't want you dancing with anyone except my daughter."

Ethan hesitated to respond. On the one hand, he didn't want to annoy the duke any more than he already had. But on the other, he didn't want the older gentleman to keep dictating his life for him either. Bracing himself for what unpleasantness might result from his reply, he said, "With all due respect, Your Grace, I don't believe you have the right to tell me who I can or can't dance with."

The duke's jaw clenched and his eye twitched. "I have every right, considering you're keeping my daughter prisoner."

"Prisoner?" If Catherine was miserable, he wouldn't have the urge to laugh at such a ridiculous statement. "Your daughter isn't a prisoner. She's with me because she wants to be. I assure you that she's happy."

"You must not mistake courage for happiness. She's always been a quiet girl, bravely accepting whatever fate has given her. She never questioned why she had to lose her mother, why she had no friends, or even why she had to marry you. Her entire life has been less than ideal. Nothing has worked in her favor, and it seems as if it never will. But I won't stand idly by while you make a fool of her. She will not have a husband who flaunts his indiscretions."

"I'm not flaunting anything because there's nothing to flaunt."

"Then there's no need to dance with anyone but her. I mean it, Lord Edon. I won't have you disgracing my daughter."

"I'm not doing anything inappropriate with Lady Richfield." How many times did he have to say it before the older gentleman believed him? And for goodness' sakes, he was dancing with her in a room full of people.

Christopher stepped up to the duke and offered a polite smile. "He's right, Your Grace. Lady Richfield and I have begun a friendly acquaintance."

The duke turned to him and narrowed his eyes at him. "You have?"

"Yes. In fact, I danced with her before Lord Edon did," Christopher replied.

"A dance doesn't prove anything."

"With all due respect, Your Grace, I believe Lord Edon was trying to tell you the same thing."

Ethan's eyebrows rose in appreciation at Christopher's reply. He was right, of course, and it delighted him that Christopher managed to twist things around on the duke so he lost the argument. If only he had such wit...

The duke's mouth twitched before he turned his cold eyes to Ethan. "I'll be watching you."

Ethan resisted the urge to roll his eyes.

As the duke walked away, Christopher shook his head at the gentleman's retreating back. "So that's your father-in-law."

"Yes. He's been a thorn in my side ever since my mother arranged the marriage. Thank you for intervening when you did. I thought for sure, he was ready to challenge me to a duel."

"Surely, you jest."

"You haven't fenced with him."

Christopher chuckled. "No, I haven't had the misfortune." He glanced over his shoulder. "Ethan, how well do you know her?"

Ethan followed his gaze to where two ladies were talking. "Who? Lady Cadwalader or Lady Richfield?"

"Lady Richfield, of course."

"Fairly well."

"Well enough to be on a first name basis?" Christopher asked, turning his attention back to Ethan.

Ethan paused. While he was good friends with Christopher, he couldn't exactly disclose the nature of his friendship with Agatha without possibly exposing her secrets, especially since their friendship involved a lot of secret meetings.

"Is the duke right to be concerned? Is there something going on between you and Lady Richfield?"

"No, there isn't anything going on. She's a friend."

"Good."

Ethan searched the room for Catherine and finally found her. She was laughing at something her father was telling her, but her father didn't seem amused. He wished he could hear their conversation. With a sigh, he said, "I happen to love my wife, even if her father can't stand the sight of me." Returning his gaze to Christopher, he saw that Christopher was smiling at Agatha who quickly looked away from him.

"I had the opportunity to dance with her," he told Ethan. "Something about her fascinates me."

"You'd be better off pursuing her sister."

"Miss Garrison?" He grimaced. "She holds no interest for me."

"Well, Lady Richfield is opposed to marriage. You'd do better to pursue another lady."

"Ethan, if there's one thing I've learned from you, it's that people are only opposed to marriage until the right person comes along. All she needs is a gentleman who'll give her a reason to want to be married."

"And you think you're that gentleman?"

"I do," Christopher said, "She's meant for me."

"She is a wealthy countess who's a widow. She has no use for an untitled gentleman who can't give her a substantial amount of money."

"But I can give her the benefit of my company," Christopher countered, looking intrigued by the challenge. "I believe she and I will be very well matched together," he added, once again turning his eyes in her direction.

Ethan snorted. "You underestimate her determination to remain unmarried."

"I don't mind proving you wrong."

"Few gentlemen are as arrogant as you, Christopher."

"Arrogant? I'm hurt." When Ethan rolled his eyes, he added, "I tell you, I am. I'm not arrogant. I'm confident."

After a long moment, Ethan said, "You're determined to be the gentleman who breaks through her wall. So what do you want me to do?"

"I want you to arrange it so that she and I will meet again."

"Dare I mention that you'll be there when I arrange this meeting?"

"I'll leave that up to you. I think she would like knowing I'd be part of this arranged meeting, but if you think a surprise is better, then I'm all for it. You know her better than I do."

Ethan thought how he might arrange such a meeting. If he had a dinner party where Agatha would be in his townhouse, his father-in-law might rest assured that he wasn't having an affair with her. No gentleman in his right mind would bring a mistress to his townhouse for a dinner party. "All right," he told Christopher. "Look for an invite in short time."

"Thank you."

Satisfied, Christopher bowed and left.

Ethan turned his attention back to Catherine, relieved when he saw her father finally leave her. Without checking to see if anyone was coming up to him, he headed for her. He came here to dance with her and to let her visit with her friends. He hadn't come to play matchmaker or be accused of infidelity. At times like this, he really wished he was at his country estate. Thankfully, in a couple months, he would be safely there.

He came up quietly behind her and tapped her shoulder. When she glanced over her shoulder, he dodged around her so that she didn't see him. Biting back a chuckle, he tapped her other shoulder, but this time she was too fast for him and caught him before he could dodge her again.

She giggled and rested her hand on his arm. "Why Lord Edon, who knew you had such a devious side to you?"

"I like to think there are a few surprises left between us," he replied with a bow. "Dance with me. I promise not to bore you."

"You could never bore me."

As he led her into a dance, he said, "I seem to remember you yawning a few times when we danced in the past."

"That was because you went into detail on what people were wearing."

"Not just any people. I was discussing the Prince Regent."

"And why would you think I cared what he was wearing?"

"Would you rather have me tell you what he was doing?"

She grimaced. "No. I suppose you were doing me a favor by saving me from that."

"Ah, so your ears are delicate after all."

Her eyebrows furrowed. "And why would you think they weren't?"

He chuckled. "Because you aren't as delicate as you pretend to be."

"I don't know if it's a matter of having delicate ears. I just don't find him interesting. He takes nothing seriously. All of life is one big ball to him. I used to think he was your hero."

"No, I just pretended he was. I saw your father talking to you."

"He wanted to make sure I'm feeling all right. I told him he'll be a grandfather earlier this week. I think he worries I might need some rest."

"How did he take the news when you told him about the child?" She seemed hesitant to respond, so he pressed, "Was he upset?"

"He's still a bit apprehensive about our marriage, but," she quickly added, "I keep assuring him everything is fine. I don't know why he won't believe me. I would've run home to him if I was miserable."

"Does he want you to return to his home?"

She lowered her gaze, and though he realized she meant to hide the truth from him, he already knew it. Her emotions were easy to decipher. "I'm not surprised," he said.

"You can't let him bother you. Sooner or later, he'll understand that I want to be with you."

He didn't share her optimism, but it was certainly nice of her to try to ease his mind. At least, things were going well between them. Forcing aside all thoughts of the duke, he returned her smile and enjoyed the rest of the evening.

Chapter Twenty-Two

"*A* dinner party?" Catherine asked from beside Ethan.

"Yes," Ethan replied as he cut into his poached egg the next morning. "I thought it might be nice. We can invite Lady Roderick, Mrs. Morris, and their husbands. What do you think?"

"It sounds lovely. Would it be a small affair?"

"As small or as big as you want. We can even invite Lady Hettinwood if Mother so desires." He glanced across the table where his mother was sipping her milk. "What do you think, Mother?"

"I don't know what you need my opinion for," his mother said, her slight smile betraying the fact that she was honored he still considered her wishes though Catherine was the countess.

"I meant what do you think of inviting Lady Hettinwood," he clarified, unable to resist teasing her. "I know you'd like to show her your porcelain doll collection."

"Oh, really, Ethan!" his mother admonished, setting her milk down and looking appropriately offended.

He shook his head and told Catherine, "Mother's been in a sour mood ever since Lady Hettinwood insisted on showing off her pottery collection."

"I haven't been in a sour mood." His mother cut into her portion of ham. "I just don't see how pottery is better than beautiful porcelain dolls, that's all."

Ethan glanced at Catherine and rolled his eyes.

Catherine giggled.

"Think what you will," his mother continued with a shrug. "It doesn't matter to me."

Clearing her throat, Catherine picked up the cloth napkin from her lap and dabbed the corners of her mouth. "I'd like to invite my father."

Ethan, who was chewing some of his egg, paused for a moment then forced himself to swallow. Even though he expected her to want the duke to come, it still made him queasy. But he had to do it. Whether he liked it or not, the duke was a permanent member of his family.

"I want him to see how happy I am," Catherine added. "Once he sees how well I'm doing here, it'll ease his mind."

"It hasn't eased his mind yet," he argued, though he realized it was pointless.

"But he hasn't seen me at a social affair in my own home," she pressed. "When he's here, he'll see us with our friends. It'll be a relaxed atmosphere."

One could only hope it would be a relaxing evening. He had to invite Agatha, and she might not enjoy him playing matchmaker, even if he was doing it reluctantly.

"I think it's a wonderful idea," his mother chimed in. "It'll be good for him."

Catherine placed her hand on Ethan's arm. While he enjoyed it when she intimately touched him, he found this type of touch—a more tender and innocent one—to be far more pleasing. It was a touch that spoke of companionship and love, something lasting and strong.

"Who will you invite?" Catherine asked him.

"Well," he began, "Mr. Robinson has always been a good friend."

"Though not a good influence," his mother commented before she bit into another piece of her ham.

"His influence is fine, Mother," he insisted. When she sighed, he turned his attention back to Catherine. "He doesn't bore me with political talk. As nice as Lord Roderick is, all he does is talk politics. Even when he plays chess, he discusses politics."

"His wife mentioned his tendency to do that."

"She's right. I hope he doesn't do it to excess when she's around."

She chuckled. "He doesn't bore her with it."

"That's good." Noting that his mother and wife were done eating, he quickly finished eating his other poached egg and wiped his mouth with his napkin. "We should adjourn to the drawing room and make a list of people we want to invite for the dinner party."

He gestured to the butler they were done and joined his wife and mother as they headed for the drawing room.

***

On the evening of the dinner party, Catherine couldn't help the butterflies fluttering around in her stomach. This was the first time she had friends—real friends—over for a formal engagement. Claire and her sister, Lilly, would be attending, and while she had visited with them a few times now, this seemed much more important. For once, she wasn't going to be at a dinner party where ladies pretended to like her because of who her father was. This time they genuinely enjoyed her company. But even though they shared a certain familiarity with each other, she still couldn't help but worry she'd say or do something to mess things up.

A knock on her bedchamber door interrupted her thoughts.

"Would you like me to answer it?" her lady's maid asked, pausing as she was brushing her hair.

Catherine looked at Opal's reflection in the vanity mirror. "Yes, please."

As Opal went to the door, Catherine took a deep breath and pinched her cheeks to give them more color. When the door opened, she saw Ethan was there and waved him in, thinking he looked wonderfully handsome. Ever since she became aware of her feelings for him, she experienced an unexpected thrill every time she saw him.

Ethan stepped into the room and shut the door while Opal went back to her and resumed brushing her hair. "You're a beautiful sight, my lady," he told her.

Her heart skipped a beat when she caught his adoring gaze. Even if he didn't say it, she sensed he loved her. Clearing her throat, she motioned to her dress. "I haven't tried wearing a russet color before."

"It's lovely on you, and I'm not just saying that so you won't change into another dress."

She grinned and glanced at Opal who picked up a few pins to put into her hair.

"Do you mind if I see what you've drawn recently?" he asked as he walked over to her daybed where she set down her drawing pad earlier that day.

"No. Go ahead." She mostly drew pictures of him, though she hid the ones of him naked in a drawer she locked. There was no need to let him know she delighted so much in exploring his body.

He picked up her drawing pad, and she turned her attention back to Opal who was finishing with her hair. After she was done, she left the room. Catherine stood up and went over to Ethan who was flipping to the last drawing in the pad.

"Don't you draw anything but me?" Ethan asked.

"I draw what interests me," she replied and kissed his cheek.

His grin widened. "And I interest you so much you draw me?"

Clasping her hands behind her back, she batted her eyelashes at him. "You're a handsome gentleman."

He reached out and drew her into his arms. She wrapped her arms around his neck and closed her eyes as he kissed her. His lips were soft and warm, his embrace protective and gentle. There was nowhere else she'd rather be.

When the kiss ended, he cupped the side of her face in his hand. "How did I ever get the fortune of marrying you?"

"It was fate."

"Fate has been very good to me."

He gave her another kiss, and she sighed in contentment.

"This dinner party means a lot to you, doesn't it?" he asked, caressing her cheek.

"I've never been to a dinner party where actual friends attended. The people who came did so because of my father."

"Well, I assure you they aren't coming because of him this time." He kissed the tip of her nose then led her to the door. "You promise me you'll protect me from your father?"

She laughed. "Surely, you're joking."

"I'm afraid not. I'm very serious."

"I wish you wouldn't give him so much thought, and since the gentlemen and ladies separate for part of the evening, I don't know how much I can do."

"Oh, yes. I will be forced to be with all the gentlemen after dinner." He winced then turned his sorrowful eyes to her as they slipped out of her bedchamber. "You will comfort me later when we're alone?"

Amused, she offered him a solemn nod. "I will do my best, my lord."

They continued down the stairs in a comfortable silence and made it to the drawing room in time for their first guests to arrive. To her delight, it was Claire and her husband. She went forward and clasped Claire's hands in hers.

"I'm so glad you could make it," she told Claire.

"I wouldn't miss it for anything," Claire replied, squeezing her hands affectionately. "You briefly spoke to my husband at our ball."

Catherine curtsied. "Thank you for coming."

Lord Roderick bowed. "It's my pleasure." Turning to Ethan, he added, "I must admit that I never thought I'd enter your townhouse."

"Yes, well, I'm afraid I have nothing of interest for you to read," Ethan teased. "At least nothing as interesting as the book I sent you shortly after you married your wife."

Catherine studied Ethan in interest, wondering what secret he shared with Claire's husband. She was under the impression the two gentlemen never spoke to each other.

Lord Roderick offered a nonchalant shrug. "One could hardly expect you to need such a book, given your only talent involves what's in it."

"Why, my lord, you flatter me so."

Catherine glanced between the gentlemen, wondering about the joke they shared that no one else did. Even Claire looked as confused as she felt.

The butler entered the drawing room. "Lady Richfield is here."

He stepped aside, and a lovely lady who had to be close to Catherine's age entered the room. When Ethan told her he was inviting her as a favor to Christopher, she hadn't concerned herself with how Lady Richfield looked. But now that she saw her, she felt a flicker of apprehension crawl up her spine. Lady Richfield was beautiful. Claire was, too, but it seemed that Claire was unaware of it. Lady Richfield, however, seemed to both know it and use it to her advantage. There was a confident air about her that made others—or at least Catherine—aware of how much they lacked.

As the butler left, Lady Richfield curtsied and offered a polite smile. "Good evening."

Ethan cleared his throat and went over to her. "We're glad you could attend the dinner party this evening. This is my wife, and these are Lord and Lady Roderick."

Forcing an uncertain smile, Catherine greeted her before Claire and Nate offered a similar greeting. The group stared at each other for a long moment, and then Ethan finally broke the awkward silence with a hesitant chuckle. As if on cue, everyone directed their gazes to him.

"Please, have a seat," he told the group. "Lady Richfield, you may have the chair over here. Lord and Lady Roderick, you may sit on the settee, and," he looked at Catherine, "you can sit on this settee with me."

Catherine nodded and sat down, feeling only slightly better when he settled next to her. She glanced at Lady Richfield who clasped her hands in her lap and made eye contact with her. Though Lady Richfield smiled, Catherine quickly averted her gaze, hoping she didn't suspect how intimidated Catherine was by her.

"Lord Roderick, what's new with the war?" Ethan asked.

Catherine would have laughed if she wasn't so nervous. Since when did Ethan concern himself with any of the wars England ever found itself engaged in?

The butler entered the drawing room again with Catherine's father. "His Grace, the Duke of Rumsey."

Catherine rose from the settee, expecting her father to come over to her, but her father glanced at Lady Richfield before he went straight over to Ethan. "If I might have a moment of your time, Lord Edon?" Though her father's tone was pleasant, she detected a subtle threat in it if Ethan didn't oblige him.

Catherine wondered if she should intervene on Ethan's behalf, but since they were in front of Lady Richfield, Claire and

Nate, she figured she better not. The last thing she wanted was for people to assume Ethan needed her to fight his battles for him. She offered Ethan an apologetic smile, knowing how much he hated talking to her father.

Ethan rose to his feet. "Of course, Your Grace. We'll talk in the library." He turned to the others and bowed. "I'll return soon."

As the two gentlemen were heading out of the room, Ethan's mother arrived. "Are the gentlemen going to another room already?" she asked.

"Not yet, Mother," Ethan replied. "His Grace requested a moment of my time. We'll return shortly."

"I hope you won't run off and leave me without an escort to the dining room, Your Grace," she told Catherine's father. "Considering the guest list, you're the only suitable one to do so."

"Oh? And who else is coming?" the duke asked.

"Mr. and Mrs. Morris and Mr. Robinson."

To Catherine's surprise, Lady Richfield's head snapped in their direction and her eyes narrowed at Ethan at the mention of Christopher's name. She wondered if Lady Richfield had guessed Ethan's intentions in inviting Mr. Robinson. If so, she wasn't pleased about it. Catherine released her breath and smoothed out the skirt of her dress. She hoped this dinner party wasn't going to turn into a disaster.

"And you can't wait until after dinner before having this private discussion with my son?" Ethan's mother pressed. "I was hoping you'd get a chance to sit and talk while we're all in the same room."

"The matter I have to discuss won't take long." The duke turned to Ethan and gestured toward the door. "After you."

Catherine winced as Ethan reluctantly obeyed her father. Granted, she knew how her father felt about him, but it didn't seem right that he should insist Ethan follow him to another room in his own townhouse, especially in front of his guests. She decided it was time to speak with her father. While he might not ever accept Ethan, he should at least allow him to be the master of his own home.

Once Ethan and her father left, Ethan's mother turned to the others in the room and grinned. "I can't remember the last time my son hosted a dinner party. I'm pleased everyone could make it. Lady Richfield, what a stunning dress you're wearing! I do so adore a rich red. You have excellent taste."

Lady Richfield relaxed and smiled. "Thank you."

"And Lord Roderick, I hear you are one of the best chess players in London," she said, turning to Claire's husband. "My son envies your skill at the game, though he'd be loathe to admit it."

Nate also seemed more comfortable. "Is that so?"

She nodded. "It is. But I think it can be our little secret." She winked. "And Lady Roderick, Catherine's told me so many good things about you. It's an honor to finally meet you."

"Oh, thank you." Claire blushed with pleasure. "Catherine's a good friend."

Catherine admired Ethan's mother. Rachel had a gift for easing the tension in any situation. It was probably something she learned after years of dealing with the many scandals Ethan created to make himself undesirable to ladies. Even so, Catherine was grateful Rachel took everyone's mind off of what just transpired between Ethan and her father. As Rachel sat in the chair next to Catherine's settee and continued talking, the others joined in the conversation. Soon, they were laughing and having a good time.

Chapter Twenty-Three

*E*than watched as his father-in-law paced the library, his hands clasped behind his back. He bit back the urge to demand the duke get it over with. He already knew why His Grace was upset, and as much as he didn't feel like hearing it, he couldn't bring himself to walk out of the room until the duke spoke his mind.

Finally, after what seemed to span an agonizing eternity, the duke turned to face him. "I will not tolerate you making a fool out of my daughter."

"I'm not making a fool out of her," Ethan replied.

His frown deepened. "Then what is Lady Richfield doing here?"

"I thought Mr. Robinson already explained his interest in her when we attended Lord and Lady Roderick's ball."

"I know very well how close you and Mr. Robinson are. I have no doubt he wished to protect you."

"Mr. Robinson is one of my friends—"

"And one who is known for getting into mischief."

Ethan resisted the urge to groan. His father-in-law was impossible to talk to. "Your Grace, if you would just listen to me, you'd realize that it's exactly as I'm saying. Mr. Robinson asked me to invite Lady Richfield here so he could get better acquainted with her. There's nothing dubious about it. I told Catherine I was inviting Lady Richfield, so she knows why she's here."

"My daughter will believe anything you tell her because she's a trusting soul. She has no reason to not believe you." After a moment of silence, he muttered, "I protected her from the undesirable ways of gentlemen such as yourself."

"I told you the truth. You can choose to accept it or not. This conversation is at an end. I have guests to tend to."

Before the duke could argue, Ethan offered a stiff bow and strode out of the library. He made it to the drawing room in time for the butler to announce Christopher's arrival. If he was lucky, he'd never have to play matchmaker again. All he needed was to further arouse his father-in-law's suspicions. It was bad enough the gentleman kept hounding him. He hadn't known a moment's peace since that fateful night he got engaged to Catherine.

He scanned the room and saw that Mr. and Mrs. Morris had arrived during his absence. Good. All the guests were here. He turned to the butler and gestured for him to arrange for everyone to go to the dining room. The sooner he got dinner started, the sooner this evening could be over.

Ignoring Catherine's father who came in behind him, he went over to Catherine and tried not to notice the uncertain expression on Agatha's face as Christopher grinned at her. He sighed. Christopher would do better if he wasn't so obvious about his interest in her. Oh well. It wasn't his problem. He had enough to deal with as it was, and the duke continued to glower at him, reminding him that he was still upset with him. Next to him, Catherine smiled. Feeling better, he returned her smile and patted the small of her back. No one would see the gesture, but he had the need to touch her, to let her know he appreciated the fact that she was nothing like her father.

The butler, mercifully, announced that dinner was ready, so the group paired off to go to the dining room. As Ethan extended his arm to Catherine, he saw Christopher make a move toward Agatha. Agatha, however, went over to the duke and looked expectantly at him, a silent maneuver on her part, Ethan knew, to let Christopher know she had no intention of letting him escort her.

Ethan's mother approached Christopher and gave him a wide smile. "It's good to see you again. I understand Lord Roderick wasn't very nice to you a couple years ago," she teased, glancing at Lord Roderick who seemed amused by her comment. "However, given how impish you used to be, I'd say that Lord Roderick did you a kindness."

At that, Lord Roderick smirked at Christopher as he and his wife passed by them on the way out of the drawing room. Since the duke had agreed to escort Agatha to dinner, Christopher had no other recourse than to extend his arm to Ethan's mother who continued to ramble on about something Ethan ignored. Ethan's main concern at this point was getting through the evening without something bad happening.

***

Two hours later, Ethan found himself sitting in his den, trying not to glance at his pocket watch as Catherine's father engaged Lord Roderick and Mr. Morris in a tedious discussion on what was happening in America. Christopher, who sat in the chair next to him, participated once in a while, but Ethan knew the topic bored him. Ethan finally gave up pretending he was interested and counted the number of times Catherine's father traced the bottom of his glass. It was a peculiar habit the duke had, and after counting thirty instances of it, Ethan had to admit it was strangely hypnotizing. He managed to get to number fifty-three when Christopher tapped his arm.

"Hmm?" Ethan glanced in his friend's direction.

"We're ready to go to the drawing room," he said, motioning to the other gentlemen who were standing by the door.

"Oh. Right." Ethan rose to his feet. "Well, then let's go." Thank goodness. The evening would soon end! While he knew the boring conversation couldn't have taken more than an hour, it had felt like an eternity.

He followed the three gentlemen to the drawing room while Christopher walked beside him. "I don't suppose I'll get a chance to be with Lady Richfield this evening?" Christopher whispered so the others wouldn't overhear.

"I told you you'd be better off pursuing her sister," Ethan whispered in return. "You'll have to make the most of whatever time we spend with the ladies for the next half hour or hour."

"I knew she was going to present a challenge, but I had no idea she'd be this difficult."

"Lady Richfield isn't one to make things easy for anyone. If you're determined to be with her, you'll have to make more of an effort. I can only do so much."

Christopher opened his mouth to respond, but they arrived in the drawing room where the ladies were talking. Lady Richfield was nowhere in sight.

"Where is Lady Richfield?" Ethan asked, already suspecting the answer but needing to verify it so Christopher would know just how much of a challenge he had ahead of him if he continued his pursuit.

"She didn't feel well, so she had to leave," Catherine replied.

"What a shame." Ethan glanced at Christopher who didn't hide his disappointment. She felt just fine, of course. Ethan knew better than to believe such a lie, but he couldn't blame her since she knew exactly why she'd been invited. With a shrug, he went to Catherine's side and sat next to her on the settee. "But there's no reason why we can't still enjoy the evening."

"Agreed," Ethan's mother replied and gestured for the gentlemen to sit down. "Perhaps we might play a game."

While the other gentlemen nodded and sat in their respective seats, Christopher gave a slight grimace before he said, "I'm afraid I have a pressing commitment early in the morning. I must take my leave."

Not surprised, Ethan rang for the butler and allowed his friend to depart before he joined the others for a game of Wit. Coming up with impromptu rhymes was much better than fretting over what the Americans were doing. By the end of the dinner party, he was laughing so hard his sides hurt.

When it was time for the guests to leave, everyone gathered in the entryway to say good-bye. Catherine's father checked his pockets. "I thought I brought my pocket watch with me this evening."

"Maybe the chain came loose and it fell off," Lord Roderick said as his carriage pulled up to the front of the townhouse.

"It's possible, I suppose," he replied.

"I'll look for it," Ethan offered, not because he was in a generous mood but because he knew the sooner the duke had it, the sooner he'd leave.

"It was a gift from my mother," Catherine told Ethan. "Maybe I should help you look for it."

"No, there's no need for that. I know where he was sitting. I'm sure it's somewhere around the chair."

As she nodded, he hurried down the hallway. He made it to the den and studied the floor as he walked over to the chair. He knelt in front of it and saw the old pocket watch lying behind it. After he picked it up, he took a moment to inspect it, surprised when he saw a crack in it. It still worked, however, but despite the fact that it was still useful, Ethan knew it was the duke's undying love for his wife that made him keep it. Touched by the gentleman's devotion, he ran his thumb along it's cracked surface. If Catherine's mother was half as lovely as Catherine, he could understand why the duke held onto her memory the way he did.

The door to the den shut behind him, and he whirled around, fully expecting the duke to demand he get away from the pocket watch at once. But it wasn't the duke who strode over to him in anger. Eyes wide, he rose to his feet and faced Agatha.

"How could you invite me here tonight with the notion of pairing me up with your friend?" she hissed, her hands on her hips.

"I thought you went home because you weren't feeling well," he whispered.

"I can't go home until I let you know how much you've upset me. After all I've done for you, you disregarded my wishes and put me in a trap. You know how much I don't want to marry."

He winced. "I know. I'm sorry." She rolled her eyes, so he quickly added, "I really am. It's just that once Christopher decides to do something, he's hard to stop. Nothing I can say will make him give up on you. He needed to be here so you could reject him to understand why he needs to pursue someone else."

"You didn't even have the decency to warn me you invited him."

"Would you have come if you knew?"

"Of course not," she grudgingly admitted, her hands falling to her sides.

"Because you came here this evening and refused to give him the chance to talk to you, you won't have to worry about him anymore."

After a long moment, she relented. "It better work."

"He's a gentleman. You hurt his pride in front of other people. He'll do everything he can to avoid you from now on."

"You think so?"

"Of course."

The door opened, and they looked at the doorway in time to see Catherine and her father staring at them. Catherine gasped and placed her hand over her mouth, and the duke clenched his hands at his sides. Ethan looked at Agatha whose jaw dropped before he turned his attention back to his wife and father-in-law.

"It isn't what it looks like," Ethan blurted out, knowing it sounded stupid as he said it. Of all things he could have been caught doing, this was the worst thing that could happen to him, especially given his reputation around the Ton.

A long, agonizing moment passed before Catherine's hand dropped. Tears filled her eyes, and she fled down the hallway.

"Catherine!" Ethan called out and hurried to the doorway.

The duke stepped in front of him and blocked his exit. "Of all the places you could have chosen for your indiscretion, you had to do it in the same townhouse my daughter lives in?"

"No. It's not an indiscretion." Ethan peered out the doorway to make sure none of the servants—or worse, his mother—saw any of this.

The duke shoved him back into the room and shut the door so the three were alone. "I knew there was something indecent going on between you and Lady Richfield as soon as I saw you dancing with her at Lord Roderick's ball. This is distasteful. Other gentlemen have the good sense to make up excuses on where they'll spend their time before running off to their mistresses."

"I don't have a mistress. Your daughter is the only one I'm with," he glanced uneasily at Agatha, not sure how he should word things in front of her but finally continued, "that way."

"Don't lie to me," the duke snapped in a hushed voice. "I'm not a simpleton. I can see what's going on here. The day my daughter married you was the worst day of my life. You don't deserve her, but she has continued to live here. God only knows why she's shown such loyalty to you. But that ends tonight. I'm taking her home with me where she'll be treated as she deserves." He pointed his finger in front of Ethan's face. "If you so much as come near my daughter again, I'll make sure we'll play a game of fencing, and I assure you, this time, there'll be an unfortunate accident. Do I make myself clear?"

The color drained from Ethan's face. Catherine wouldn't go home with her father, would she? She'd at least give him a chance to explain, to try to make things right. Wouldn't she?

The duke snatched the pocket watch from Ethan's hand. "I trust you'll find a way to keep your mistress out of sight so the servants won't know of my daughter's shame." He glared at Agatha before he spun on his heel and stormed out of the room.

It took Ethan a second before he could act. Not waiting for Agatha to say anything, he ran after the duke who was heading for the butler who was carrying a tray out of the drawing room.

"I demand to talk to my daughter at once," the duke told the butler, his tone resolute.

"No, he won't," Ethan countered.

"You have no right to tell me I won't talk to her," he snapped, his face getting red with anger.

"I have every right. This is my townhouse, and that's my butler. You are not at liberty to make such demands here. And whether you like it or not, Catherine's not going anywhere. She's my wife. Though you don't believe it, I love her. I would never do anything to hurt her."

"A gentleman such as yourself doesn't know the first thing about love. She was my daughter long before she became your wife. I've spent years taking care of her."

"The length of time you've been with someone has nothing to do with the depth of your feelings for them."

"Maybe not, but I believe a person with your reputation is incapable of the kind of love someone like my daughter deserves." He turned to the butler. "Send for Lady Catherine at once."

"She's not Lady Catherine!" Ethan gestured for the butler to remain still and faced the duke, squaring his shoulders back. This confrontation was a long time in coming, and he decided if he was going to take his stand, he was going to do it for the sake of his marriage. "She is Lady Edon. She is a countess. Because of that, she will remain here."

The duke stepped up to him, his nose just inches from Ethan's, and narrowed his eyes at him. "I call a duel."

"You can't call a duel. It's illegal."

He stared at him, so Ethan stared right back, refusing to blink. The moment was tense between them. Neither moved nor spoke. The entire place fell deathly silent.

Finally, the butler cleared his throat and, in a tentative tone, said, "Your Grace, my duty is to Lord Edon. Lady Edon will remain here until he says she can go or unless she decides to go of her own free will. I will not intervene on your behalf."

The duke gritted his teeth and kept on staring at Ethan.

Though his heart was pounding, Ethan forced out, "This evening's entertainment is at an end." He scanned the hallway and saw that the footman had been standing behind him. "Make sure His Grace gets to his carriage."

The footman rushed to the front door and opened it.

Catherine's father shifted his gaze from Ethan, to the butler, to the footman, and back to Ethan. "She won't stay here. She'll leave of her own accord."

"That remains to be seen," Ethan replied, hoping she wouldn't once he explained everything to her.

He let out a low grunt and stormed out the front door.

Ethan knew he should be relieved his father-in-law was gone, and yet he wasn't. Confronting the duke should have been the hardest part of this evening, but it wasn't. His gaze went to the stairs. The hardest part was going to be begging Catherine to stay with him. She'd been devastated to find him alone in the den with Agatha. Even with all the tears she'd cried on their wedding day, he hadn't seen her this upset.

She loved him. He hadn't realized it until he saw how deeply he'd hurt her. Well, he loved her, too. But he also understood as innocent as his talk with Agatha had been, the fact that he was caught in the den alone with another lady was enough to do damage he never wanted to do. He needed to do whatever it took to make things right. Taking a deep breath, he headed up the stairs, not bothering to look at the footman or the butler.

Chapter Twenty-Four

Catherine sat in the chair next to the vanity in her bedchamber and wiped the tears from her eyes with her handkerchief. She shouldn't be surprised. Even if Ethan hadn't been with a lady before he married her, gentlemen often took mistresses. Why should she expect her husband to be any different? Though she loved him, it didn't mean he loved her, and even if he did, would that prevent him from still wanting to take a mistress?

She wiped her eyes again. If she didn't love him, she wouldn't care. But since she did love him, it hurt to think he needed more than what she could give him, especially when she'd given him everything she had to offer anyone. She'd felt safe to let down her guard with him, and that made her all the more vulnerable.

A soft tap at her door drew her attention to it. Assuming it was Opal, she called out for her to enter. But instead of Opal, Ethan opened the door and stepped into the room. She quickly averted her gaze from him in case she broke into a fresh wave of tears. She didn't want him to know how much he could hurt her. That would be worse than fleeing the way she did when she caught Ethan alone with Lady Richfield, probably discussing when they'd take time to be more intimate.

Ethan shut the door and took a hesitant step toward her. "Catherine?"

Refusing to look at him, she focused on the mirror in front of her and twisted the edge of the handkerchief around one of her fingers. She cleared her throat and prayed her voice would come out sounding neutral. If she could convince him she didn't care, she could save what little dignity she had left. "What do you want?"

To her surprise, he knelt beside her and touched her hand. "It wasn't what it looked like, Catherine," he said, his tone so tender she couldn't help but make eye contact with him. "I should have told you about Agatha sooner, but I knew she wouldn't like it so I didn't."

"You refer to her by her Christian name?"

He sighed. "It's not what you think. Agatha is a friend, but we've kept our friendship a secret because if others found out why we even have an acquaintance, it would ruin her reputation."

Catherine considered his words carefully before she replied. "Does this acquaintance you share involve love?"

"No. I don't love her. I love you."

"You do?"

He brought her hand to his lips and kissed it. "There will only be you, Catherine. I will never have a mistress. As long as I am with you, I am complete."

She examined his eyes and saw that he was telling her the truth. She wrapped her arms around his neck and brought her lips to his. The sorrow just moments before was quickly forgotten as he deepened their kiss. In her heart, she knew her love was secure with him, that he would love her the way her father had loved her mother. And she couldn't think of anything better than that.

When the kiss ended, she ventured, "Why do you have an acquaintance with Agatha?"

After a moment of silence, he cupped her face in his hands, his thumbs gentle as they traced her cheeks. "I don't think she'd mind if I told you since you're my wife and won't tell anyone. Agatha is a writer. She writes gothic horror, but those in her family wouldn't accept it if they knew, so she decided to write under the name of a gentleman. But she can't go to Minerva Press and submit her story because she knows the publisher. Even if she dresses up as a gentleman, she's afraid he'll recognize her."

"She disguises herself as a gentleman?" Catherine asked, appalled a lady would do such a thing.

"Only if she has to. She also has taken the role of a gentleman when she writes for the *Tittletattle*."

"She's one of the authors for the scandalsheets?" While she could understand why Agatha would hide her identity for gothic horror, she couldn't understand why Agatha would write gossip. "Why did she get involved with the *Tittletattle?*"

"Because she wanted to do something no one would accept if they knew."

"I don't understand."

He kissed her nose and smiled. "She was bored. She had just gone through her first Season where she had to be a perfect lady at all times. Then she was married and widowed within twenty-four hours and felt that her life had no meaning. She didn't wish to marry, and when she realized she wasn't with child, she decided to take a chance and do something she found entertaining. Her first notion was to write a book, which she did, but then it isolated her. While she doesn't engage often in social affairs because she doesn't want to remarry, she gets lonely. When she disguises herself as a gentleman and contributes to the *Tittletattle*, she is connected to the world."

"So how did you two meet?"

"I happened to catch her in her disguise as a gentleman and noticed her mustache was falling off." He chuckled and rose to his feet. Taking her hands in his, he helped her up. "In return for my silence on the matter, she made up stories about me in the *Tittletattle*. As we got to know each other, I started submitting her stories to the publisher."

"Are you saying all of the gossip about you wasn't true?"

"Well, I did win every game at White's and the gambling hells, but everything else was a lie."

"I don't understand, Ethan. Why did you go through all that trouble of lying so you'd seem like a rake?"

He shrugged. "I had convinced myself that I wanted to stop coming to London so I could enjoy a quiet and peaceful life in the country. Having spent time with you, however, I think the truth of the matter is that I was afraid."

"Afraid of what?"

"Afraid I wouldn't be happy if I was married. My mother and father were happy. With so few marriages being like theirs, I didn't think I would have the fortune of having a wife who'd love me and who I'd love back. It was safer to convince my mother to pass on my title to my cousin so I wouldn't have to worry about having an heir. Then I wouldn't have to marry at all."

Touched by his confession, she softly replied, "I love you, Ethan."

With a smile, he lowered his head and kissed her.

As much as she wanted to melt in his arms and let the rest of the world slip away, there was one thing that bothered her. "Ethan, what were you and Agatha doing in the den?"

"She wasn't pleased that I invited Christopher to the dinner party. She knew that I was trying to play matchmaker."

"I saw her face when he arrived, and she didn't look happy."

"Well, maybe now he'll understand that she's not interested in him and find another lady to pursue."

"Maybe."

"You don't think he will give up his pursuit of Agatha?"

She shrugged. "I don't know, really. It's just that from what Claire told me about him, he's not the kind of gentleman who gives up once he sets his mind to something. But he's your friend. You know him better than she does." Deciding they'd talked enough about Christopher and Agatha, she said, "Why don't you retire to your bedchamber, and after I have Opal help me get ready for bed, I'll join you. I know how much this room bothers you," she added in a playful tone.

"Sometimes lace and ruffles are distracting."

She giggled at the way he grimaced and kissed him. "I don't mind spending the nights with you in your bedchamber. Now, let me tend to my needs, so I can be with you again."

He gave her an affectionate pat on the small of her back and left the room. Her spirits lifted, she pulled the cord to let Opal know she was ready for her and got to work on pulling the pins out of her hair. Opal arrived shortly after she started brushing her hair and helped her undress. Once she was in her shift and robe, she thanked Opal. Opal curtsied and left. Unable to hide her excitement over seeing Ethan again, especially since she knew he loved her, she knocked on the door separating their bedchambers.

"I was beginning to think you decided not to come," he teased, reaching for her hand and pulling her into his arms.

She didn't have time to reply, for he was kissing her once more. To her delight, he picked her up and carried her to his bed where he'd already pulled the covers back. It was wonderful to know he had chosen her—and only her—to take to his bed. He gently set her down and settled next to her.

Lowering his head, he brought his mouth to hers and traced the length of her body with his hand. She ran her fingers through the silky strands of his hair. After he untied the cord holding her robe together, he ran his hand over her shift, delighting her as he brushed her breasts, lightly teasing her nipples, which hardened in response. Then his hand lowered, traveling down her side, over her hip and to the edge of her shift.

She squirmed beside him, eager to have him explore her more intimately. He obeyed her silent wish and slid his hand under her shift then between her legs. She widened her legs for him and lifted her hips to grant him better access to her sensitive flesh. His fingers brushed her entrance. She shivered in pleasure and brought her lips to his cheek and then his neck.

"You feel good," he murmured as his thumb settled on her sensitive nub.

She softly moaned, still kissing his neck, her body aching for him to penetrate her. "Please, slip your fingers into me," she whispered.

He did as she requested, and she adjusted her hips so that he was deeper inside her. As he stroked her core, she squeezed his arms. Her body responded so easily to him. He knew exactly how to touch her, ensuring that she would climax. And when she did, she cried out his name, closing her eyes and savoring the moment as he continued to stroke her, his fingers gentle, his rhythm slower than it had been before.

When she was satisfied, she slipped his fingers out of her and rolled onto her knees so that she could remove her robe and shift. Then she helped him out of his nightclothes. She encouraged him to lie on his back and took a moment to study his body, thrilled that he was aroused simply by being with her in bed. She loved knowing she could get him hard, that he desired her physically. Before she got married, she had no idea the marital bed could bring so much pleasure, nor did she understand that becoming one with her husband would give her such a feeling of completion. But with Ethan, it was easy to be vulnerable and know she was safe with him.

Making eye contact with him, she smiled and winked before she knelt in front of him. She took his erection in her hand and stroked it, working her way from the base to the tip, her finger tracing the bead of moisture at the slit. He groaned in pleasure and grasped the sheets beneath him. She took him into her mouth and traced his tip with her tongue. He murmured her name and squirmed in pleasure as she continued her ministrations.

As much as she loved receiving pleasure from their lovemaking, the act was more complete when he found fulfillment in it, too.

When he whispered that he couldn't hold out much longer, she straddled him and took him inside her. He placed his hands on her hips and guided her movements. She rocked back and forth on top of him, her body clenching around him, her sensitive nub rubbing against him in such a way that further aroused her. She worked with him, striving for the same goal as he was, and as she climaxed once more, he joined her, his seed filling her, bringing completion to the act. She remained still on top of him, waiting for the last waves of pleasure to subside before opening her eyes.

When he looked at her, he smiled so tenderly at her that her heart melted. "Thank you," he whispered, giving her hips a gentle squeeze.

"I received pleasure from this, too," she replied.

"No, I didn't mean this. Though this is definitely one of the best things I've ever experienced. I meant thank you for believing me about Agatha. I realize how things looked. Your father wanted to take you away from me tonight. If you left with him, I don't know what I would have done. I can't imagine my life without you."

She cupped his face in her hands and kissed him. "You'll never have to be without me, Ethan. I'm not going anywhere."

His smile widened as he embraced her and gave her another kiss. And it wasn't too long before they were making love again.

Chapter Twenty-Five

Catherine's father, Enoch, had a restless night's sleep, and he barely managed to eat breakfast. All he kept seeing in his mind was his daughter running away from the den. She'd been devastated. Maybe a part of it was his fault. He did everything he could to shelter Catherine from the harsher realities of life, and though they both knew what kind of gentleman Ethan was before she married him, he hadn't taken the time to sit her down and warn her that someone like Ethan didn't have the decency to hide his scandalous behaviors.

Enoch paced his library, trying to think of how he might rescue his daughter since Ethan refused to let her leave his prison. Of all the sins Ethan took part in, he never imagined that holding a lady in his home against her will was on the list. Enoch silently cursed himself. This disaster was his doing. He should have been forceful. He should have shoved Ethan aside and climbed those stairs to get to his daughter. He shouldn't have left Ethan's townhouse.

Why did he leave? Even as he asked himself the question, he knew the answer. He hadn't expected Ethan to stand his ground. In the past, Ethan had been afraid of him. It was that fear that gave Enoch the advantage. But his son-in-law wasn't afraid of him anymore.

Grimacing, he clenched his hands behind his back and went to the window, his gaze going in the direction where his poor little girl was, trapped and miserable. He had to find some way of talking to her. She was his daughter, and he had every right to get her out of that townhouse. He'd spent enough time worrying about her. It was time to barge into that townhouse and force Ethan to let him see his daughter, and if it took a smallsword to get Ethan to comply, then so be it.

Feeling better now that he had a plan, Enoch hurried out of the room and up the stairs. He'd rescue Catherine if it was the last thing he did. As soon as he entered his bedchamber, he headed for the cord to let his valet know he was ready to change his clothes when a hooded figure emerged from his armoire.

His first thought was that it was Ethan, but upon closer inspection, he realized that the person was shorter and thinner than Ethan. It couldn't be Catherine. Catherine wouldn't hide under a hooded cloak to see him. Furrowing his eyebrows, he barked, "Who are you?"

The person pulled back the hood.

His jaw dropped. "Lady Richfield?"

Lady Richfield offered him a nod and sat on his bed as if it was the most natural thing in the world for her to do. "I believe you have me in a vulnerable situation, Your Grace."

"I have *you* in a vulnerable situation? May I remind you that you're the one who snuck into my townhouse and hid in my bedchamber?"

With a shrug, she clasped her hands and put them on her lap. "If your valet were to walk through the door, would it matter?" She made eye contact with him, her eyebrows arched in a silent challenge.

"You're obviously here for a reason, and since you're with my son-in-law, I doubt it's any good."

"I'm not with him in the sense that you mean. I came here to demonstrate how easy it is to misunderstand a situation.

If your valet, or another servant, were to come in here at this moment, they would assume we're about to engage in a rather interesting activity, wouldn't you agree?"

"They would only assume that because of the room we're in."

"And if we were in another room...say a library or the drawing room?"

"Then it wouldn't be an issue."

"It wouldn't? Even though you are a gentleman and I am a lady?"

He resisted the urge to groan. It seemed to him that Lady Richfield was playing with him as a cat played with a mouse. "Will you please get to the point?"

"My point is that I was with Lord Edon in the den. I wasn't in his bedchamber. And yet you assumed something of a personal nature was transpiring between us. But if I was with you in the den, then you expect everyone to believe it was innocent."

"I don't have the reputation that Lord Edon does," he replied, not enjoying the triumphant look she had on her face. She was baiting him, and he got the feeling he was falling into her trap.

"Neither do I. Do you recall anything scandalous involving me?"

"No."

"So why did you assume I was his mistress?"

Growing impatient, he said, "Because you were with him and he's well-known for having mistresses."

She rose to her feet and approached him. "Your Grace, I am not the kind of lady who would degrade herself by being someone's mistress. A mistress doesn't stand to inherit a gentleman's money, and if she has his child, that child is illegitimate. I know better than to give my body to anyone unless I can be assured I'll receive his money and that my son will one day inherit his title. My marriage might have been brief, but I'm a countess and have more than enough money to see me to my death. Given that, why would I be Lord Edon's mistress?"

"Because you wanted to be intimate with him," he replied.

To his surprise, she started laughing. "The physical act of intimacy might be enjoyable to gentlemen, but it isn't so for ladies."

"That's not true." As soon as he said those words, he cursed himself. It wasn't any of her business what his marriage had been like.

She continued to chuckle. "Since you are a gentleman, you have to believe that ladies enjoy the act, or can at least tolerate it. But I'm not here to argue how wrong you are about that. I'm here to explain why you're wrong about Lord Edon and me. What Lord Edon and I have is a friendship. Due to certain circumstances, we've kept the friendship a secret."

"Is that so?"

"Yes, it is so," she replied in a tone that indicated she was about to win the argument—and he didn't like that at all. She turned from him, walked a couple steps from him, and turned back to face him with her hands on her hips. "I have a few secrets I don't want anyone else to know, but you are so stubborn, I'll tell you what they are. I am a writer. I write for the *Tittletattle*, and I write gothic horror. I do the two under the names of two gentlemen. Lord Edon has been gracious about submitting my stories to the publisher, and in return, I have spread gossip for him in the *Tittletattle*."

Enoch couldn't believe his ears. "Why would you spread gossip about him?"

"Because he asked me to. He hoped to avoid marriage if enough scandals kept mothers from throwing their daughters at him." Scanning him up and down, she added, "You didn't strike me as a gentleman who believed everything he read in the scandalsheets. I thought you had more sense than that."

"I don't care for the way you're talking to me. I'm not a child."

"And I don't care for the way you treated Lord Edon yesterday. He told you the truth, and you refused to believe him. He loves your daughter and wouldn't do anything to hurt her. From what I saw at the dinner party, he's very happy with her. And what's more, she's also happy with him. The two are well matched. If you won't believe what he has to say, then at least listen to your daughter. You should be able to determine whether she's telling you the truth or not if you take the time to really listen to what she's saying. Too many times, people assume they're hearing one thing when the person talking is saying something else."

As much as he was loath to admit it, she had a point. Catherine kept assuring him she was fine, that she was happy with Ethan. He assumed she said it only to ease his guilt. But if what Lady Richfield said was true, if Ethan was faithful to Catherine, then he at least owed Ethan a chance.

Lady Richfield pulled the hood of her cloak up to hide her identity. "I trust this conversation will remain between you and me."

"I'd be a fool to mention it since you were in my bedchamber when it happened," he replied, sensing that was why she picked this very room to talk to him in. "Just how did you get in here undetected anyway?"

She pulled back the edge of her hood and gave him a wink. "A lady never tells her secrets."

He rolled his eyes. Of course, she wouldn't answer the question. He watched as she opened his door a crack, waited for a few seconds, and slipped into the hallway. Deciding it would be best to give her ample time to sneak out of his townhouse, he changed his own clothes instead of calling for the valet.

***

Ten minutes later, Catherine stood in her father's drawing room as she waited for the butler to find him. She knew the previous evening didn't look well to her father. It hadn't looked well to her either at the time. She wasn't sure what she would tell him about Agatha and Ethan's friendship. She had promised to keep Ethan's secrets, and she would. In this case, her father would have to trust her.

Taking a deep breath, she faced the portrait of her mother. She placed her hands over her abdomen, mindful of the baby even though she wasn't showing yet. If she had a girl, she'd like to name the child after her mother. The past couple of months had marked significant changes in her life. She was finally a wife and had a child on the way. At the beginning of the year, she didn't think her life could turn out so differently, but she was glad it did.

Footsteps caught her attention, and she turned in time to see her father stride toward her. "I was ready to go to your husband's townhouse and see you," he said, scanning the room. "Is he here?"

With a sigh bordering on amusement, she went over to him and hugged him. "No, he didn't come. He wanted to, but I told him I wanted to talk to you alone." Pulling away from him, she motioned to the settee.

"Do you want to come back home?" he softly asked, studying her face. "If you do, say the word and you never have to go back to him."

"Father," she began, fighting down the frustration that she often experienced when he insisted she had to be miserable with Ethan. She took his arm and led him to the settee. She sat down and waited for him to sit beside her. Clasping her hands in her lap, she turned toward him. "I'm happy where I am."

The butler came into the room with a tray of tea and biscuits. After he set it on the table in front of them, she smiled her thanks to the butler who bowed and left, shutting the door behind him.

She poured tea for her father before pouring it into her cup. "Why can't you accept that I want to be with Ethan?"

A long pause elapsed between them as he rubbed his knees. "You were upset last night. Aren't you still upset today?"

"I was upset last night, but then Ethan explained everything to me. Lady Richfield isn't his mistress."

"And you believe him?"

She picked up her cup and set it in her lap. "I do. Deep down inside, I know he wouldn't do anything to hurt me." When she noted the way his eyebrows furrowed, she shook her head. "I can't explain it. It's just a feeling I have."

"So what did he tell you about last night? Why was he talking to Lady Richfield?"

"I can't tell you."

He grunted.

"I'm sorry, but I can't. I know it sounds like something is wrong because I can't explain it to you, but I promised him I'd honor him by keeping his secrets. Father," she placed her cup back on the tray and reached for his hands, gently squeezing them, "can't you trust me to know what's best for me?"

His expression grew soft and he squeezed her hands in return. "You're right, Catherine. I should trust you." He paused. "You really are happy?"

"Yes."

He released her hands and let out a long sigh. "I suppose it's time I stopped thinking of you as a little girl who needs protecting and accept the fact that you're a grown lady."

She smiled. "I don't mind it if you protect me. Just as long as you understand Ethan also wants to protect me. You two are very important to me, and I'd like for you to get along. Can you please try to see Ethan for who he is instead of what his reputation says about him?"

"I can't promise you that I'll like him, but I will try."

"Thank you."

It was all she could ask of him, and since he was finally accepting the fact that she was happy with Ethan, she felt much better about the future.

***

Late February 1816
Lord and Lady Edon's Country Estate

Catherine gave her father a hug as soon as he walked through the front door. "I'm so glad you came!"

"Of course I came," he replied and kissed her cheek. "How is my granddaughter?"

"She's doing well." She turned and saw Ethan's mother as she brought the baby girl over to them. "Ethan and I decided to name her Audrey."

Her father took the week-old baby in his arms and stroked her cheek. "You named her after your mother?"

"I thought it would be a good way to carry on her memory."

"It's a lovely way to remember her," he whispered, his smile widening. "She's so small. I don't remember you being this small, but you had to be."

"All babies are small when they're born," Ethan's mother spoke up. "And thank goodness for that or mothers everywhere would be in trouble."

Catherine couldn't argue with Rachel's statement. She was still sore from giving birth, and though Audrey seemed like a big baby when she was still in her womb, Catherine had to admit she was tiny when she first held her. But as her gaze fell to her child, Catherine couldn't help but think she'd go through childbirth all over again just to have her. Glancing over her shoulder at Ethan who stood away from the group, she waved him over.

"I think we'd be more comfortable in the drawing room," Ethan said.

"Oh, he's right," Rachel replied and motioned for everyone to follow her. Looking at the duke, she added, "We'll have your things brought in shortly, Your Grace."

After they entered the drawing room, Ethan took Catherine's arm and helped her get comfortable on the settee. Catherine's father sat in the chair across from them, not too far from the chair Ethan's mother chose to sit in.

"This is so wonderful," Rachel cheered, clapping her hands in excitement. "I just knew this is what it'd be like when we arranged the marriage. Audrey is a fortunate little girl to be born into this home."

"Are you sure you're not disappointed that you didn't have a grandson?" Ethan asked as the butler brought in a tray of tea and biscuits. "Audrey won't be able to inherit my title."

"Oh, that's easy to take care of," she said. She picked up the teapot and began pouring tea into everyone's cups as the butler left the room. "You and Catherine will have to keep having children until you have a son."

"And if we don't? We could have thirty or more girls and never have a son."

Catherine's eyes grew wide. "Thirty or more girls?"

Ethan glanced at her. "It's possible."

She accepted the cup his mother offered her. "I don't think so, Ethan. We might have all girls, but there's no need to exaggerate their number."

Catherine's father chuckled and turned his tender eyes to her. "All you really need is one to be complete."

Catherine smiled, pleased he chose to give her such a high compliment.

"Tell me, Your Grace," Ethan began after he took a sip of his tea, "did you have a good journey?"

"I did. The weather cooperated with me." He arched an eyebrow and added, "I even brought my fencing gear, if you're so inclined to take the risk."

Ethan smirked. "You're in for a rude awakening. I've been practicing. I dare say I might be good enough to have you running out of the room."

Catherine's father laughed, the twinkle in his eye indicating that he enjoyed the challenge Ethan gave him. "Somehow I doubt that."

"Then we'll have to see, won't we?"

Ethan's mother bit into a biscuit, swallowed, and wiped her mouth with a cloth napkin. "I think we can tell them now," she told Catherine's father.

Catherine took a sip of her tea and glanced at Ethan to see if he had any idea what his mother meant. Since he shrugged, she asked, "Tell us what?"

"Well," his mother began with a slight blush, "we wanted to wait until after Audrey was born to tell you the good news. Catherine, your father and I began a correspondence once we left London."

"Actually, she sent the first one," her father clarified.

"It was only to assure him that you were doing fine," she added. "He sent me a correspondence in return, and soon I realized that we had a lot in common."

"Oh no," Ethan muttered, his face going white.

Eyebrows furrowed, Catherine studied him, wondering why he looked afraid of what his mother would say next. Turning her attention back to Rachel, she pressed, "So what's this news?"

"Your father and I are getting married when we go back to London!" his mother announced. "Isn't that wonderful?"

Ethan swallowed the lump in his throat, and though he moved his mouth, no words came out.

Resisting the urge to giggle at Ethan's reaction, Catherine nodded. "It is wonderful. You two will do very well together."

"I told you they'd be happy for us," his mother told her father before directing her attention back to Catherine and Ethan. "After the marriage, I'll live with His Grace, of course, but that doesn't mean we won't still see each other. We'll want to visit our granddaughter and any other grandchildren you'll give us."

"Even if there's thirty of them," Catherine's father teased.

"Though," Ethan's mother quickly added, "you'll have to allow us some time alone right after we marry so we can get to know each other better."

Ethan, who'd been ready to eat a biscuit, shuddered and tossed it back onto the tray. "Mother, please! I'll never eat again if you add anything else to that statement."

His mother shook her head. "I don't understand why such talk should bother you. It's not like you're innocent to the ways of the world."

He clasped his hands over his ears. "If you won't stop talking for my sake, will you do it for your granddaughter's?"

"To be fair," she countered, "it took you time to be alone with Catherine to get my granddaughter."

Catherine giggled when Ethan groaned. She tried so hard not to laugh, but given the fact that his mother and her father still thought he used to be a rake, his reaction to his mother's bold talk was too much for her to handle.

"Rachel, the day is pleasant enough to take our granddaughter for a walk," Catherine's father said. "Do you mind if we take Audrey out, Catherine? We won't be gone long, and we'll be sure to bundle her up."

"I think it's a good idea, Father," Catherine replied.

Ethan rubbed his eyes and muttered something under his breath as the two left the room.

Curious, Catherine placed her hand on his shoulder and leaned into him. "Are you really horrified that our parents are getting married?"

Letting out a weary sigh, he dropped his hands to his sides and looked at her. "How can those two be happy together? My mother has little sense of decency when she talks, and your father holds so rigidly to propriety."

"I suspect they'll balance each other out, much like we do."

He grimaced.

"It's true, Ethan. We complement each other very well. You bring out the more exciting part of me, one I never knew existed until I married you. And I bring out the part of you that wants to be a reputable gentleman, something you fought hard to avoid before you married me."

"Well…that's true."

"I think we're better together than we are apart."

"I can't argue that," he replied.

"And they will benefit each other the same way. My father closed himself off to love after my mother died. He wouldn't remarry because he couldn't imagine enjoying another lady's companionship. But your mother will make that part of him live again."

"And my mother? What does she have to gain from such a union?" Ethan asked.

"She'll be loved as a lady desires to be loved. Children are a blessing, but there's something about having the love of an honorable gentleman that makes a lady feel complete." She reached for his hand and kissed him. "They'll make a good match, Ethan, just like we do."

Relaxing, he grinned. "We do make a good match, don't we?"

"No one could be matched any better."

His smile widening, he kissed her again. She wrapped her arms around his neck and pulled him closer to her. He deepened the kiss, and the rest of the world faded away as she gave into the bliss of being with her husband.

Already Available in the Regency Collection…

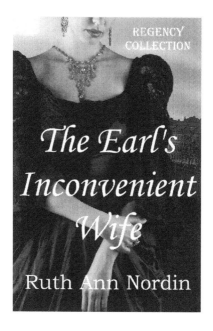

Caught in a scandalous situation, Lord Roderick marries a lady he believes tricked him into marriage. Miss Claire Lowell hoped her first Season would result in a marriage based on love, but her new husband hates her. Can she convince him she didn't trick him into marriage or will she be confined to the loveless marriage she fears?

Her Counterfeit Husband

RUTH ANN NORDIN

The Duchess of Watkins' husband just died, and her unscrupulous brother-in-law is ready to step in as the Duke of Watkins. In desperation, the duchess enlists the help of the butler, and the two agree to quietly bury her husband and pretend he's still alive. It will be a secret they will take to their graves.

After burying him in a forest, they come across a gentleman who has been beaten and left for dead. And this gentleman happens to look exactly like her husband. Seeing this as the answer to their prayers, they take him home in hopes he'll agree to be the new Duke of Watkins. There's only one problem. When he wakes up, he doesn't remember who he is.

Dare they replace her husband with a counterfeit? And if they do, what consequences will come as a result of their lie?

Made in the USA
Lexington, KY
14 August 2013